ODYSSEUS
IN THE
SERPENT
MAZE

YOUNG HEROES

ODYSSEUS
IN THE
SERPENT
MAZE

By
JANE YOLEN
and
ROBERT J. HARRIS

SCHOLASTIC INC.

New York Toronto London Auckland Sydney
Mexico City New Delhi Hong Kong Buenos Aires

ISBN 0-439-52038-X

12 11 10 9 8 7 6 5 4 3 2 1   3 4 5 6 7 8/0

Printed in the U.S.A.   40

First Scholastic printing, January 2003

To the Harris boys:
Matthew, Robert, and Jamie,
heroes all

Contents

CHAPTER ONE

HUNTING
THE BOAR

"Odysseus! Odysseus! Where are you?"

Beads of sweat ran down the boy's face as he called. His tunic—white when he had started the climb and now a moist gray—clung to his scrawny back. His padded linen leggings were scuffed and torn. He had lost his hat some time back.

Above him loomed the double peaks of Parnassus, a faint glint of snow visible on the heights. Just the glimpse of the snow made him feel cold, and he shivered. In the light of early dawn long, jagged shadows lanced out from rocks and trees. That, too, made him tremble.

He was about to call again when he felt a tug at the

hem of his tunic, then a yank, and suddenly he was pulled forward, off his feet, his face ground into the grass.

"Mentor," came a harsh whisper, "if you can't keep up, at least keep quiet!"

Spitting out a blade of grass, Mentor sat up and glared at Odysseus, who was crouching beside him, a long spear clutched in his hand.

"I tried to keep up, but you were going too fast." Mentor set down his own javelin and checked himself all over for bruises. "And I still don't understand why we couldn't wait till after breakfast. I have no strength for climbing when my belly is empty."

Odysseus never looked at his friend but kept scanning the bushes and the scruffy ground between trees. "My grandfather says it's best to track an animal first thing in the morning, while it's—"

"—sluggish," Mentor finished for him. "I remember. But I also remember your father warning me: 'Keep Odysseus out of trouble, because it is as certain as Hades his grandfather will not.'"

Odysseus' face got as red as his hair. "I'm not in trouble."

"You will be," Mentor said smugly, "when your grandfather finds out you took his prize hunting spear!"

Only then did Odysseus turn, his broad face marred with a crease that ran between his eyebrows. Someone else might think that was a worry line. But Mentor had known Odysseus since childhood. That line was a sign that Odysseus was about to come up with an outlandish excuse—lie, fib, wile—for doing something he'd already decided to do. He'd call it a *reason*, of course, but reason was the one thing it wouldn't be.

"The spear was just hanging there in Grandfather's storeroom gathering dust," Odysseus said. "In the midst of all those old shaggy pelts and moldy tusks, and piles of copper and gold." He grinned. "Besides, Grandfather always did admire a nimble bit of thieving. That's what *he's* famous for, after all!"

"Your own javelin would have done as well," said Mentor, sighing. "That spear is much too big for you."

In fact the spear was a good two feet longer than Odysseus, and he could barely stretch his fingers around the shaft. But he wasn't going to admit that to Mentor. Instead he shrugged. The vertical line between his brows got deeper.

"You need a proper weapon to slay a beast like the Boar of Parnassus, not a sewing needle like yours." Odysseus glanced disdainfully at Mentor's javelin. "Besides, I don't plan to throw the spear from any great distance. There's nothing heroic in that. We'll make the boar come right up to us."

Mentor stood and brushed off his clothes. "This is a bad idea, Odysseus." He looked around at the scrub bushes, perfect hiding places for wild animals. "We should have a whole hunting party with us, with hounds and—"

"So the dogs can do the hunting for us and the *real* men run ahead, and we don't even get a glimpse of the quarry till the hunt is all over?" Odysseus stood as well. In perfect imitation of one of his grandfather's servants, he said in a high, breathy voice, "Oh, Prince Odysseus, it's too dangerous. You don't want to stain your fine tunic. You're too small to handle the great big grown-up spear. You're *only* thirteen years old!"

Odysseus said the last with such scorn, Mentor bowed his head, resigned to the fact that he'd already lost this argument an hour ago, when Odysseus had shaken him awake on his sleeping pallet. But he hoped to inject at least a small note of caution into their adventure. Anything to keep Odysseus safe—in spite of himself.

"How are we going to find this boar?" Mentor asked.

"I think we already have." Odysseus knelt again and yanked Mentor down after him. "Smell that!"

Mentor sniffed but smelled nothing unusual. "I don't—"

"Shhhhh!" Odysseus' angry hiss silenced him.

They got down on their bellies and slid through the undergrowth, Odysseus in the lead.

I hope, Mentor thought, *that my tunic can be mended. I am not so sure about my knees.*

The bushes all seemed to have thorns, and the crawl took a long time. Mentor knew better than to complain again. He didn't want to face more of Odysseus' withering scorn. But at last they got through to the other side of the brambles. Odysseus squatted and signaled with his hand for Mentor to do the same.

"There—see that goat trail?"

Mentor squinted. "Yes—so?"

"There in the middle. Boar spoor. A whole pile of it."

Mentor wrinkled his nose. *Now* he could smell it.

"Fresh, too," Odysseus said. "Probably his first of the day."

"You're certain it's the right beast?" Mentor asked. Like Odysseus, he'd never actually been on a boar hunt, only heard the boasts of men when they had drunk too much wine at a feast. But he knew a boar was a fast beast and, when angered or even just slightly annoyed, a boar could be deadly.

"Deer keep free of these trails," Odysseus said with great authority, though there was that deep line between his eyes again. "And the spoor is too big for sheep or goat." He eased himself back into the bushes. Mentor did the same.

"You can't be completely sure. . . ." Mentor didn't want to believe Odysseus. He didn't want to encounter a real boar. Not now, with only his small javelin. His "sewing needle." Not on such a lovely summer day. Not—

"There are lots of birds' nests in these bushes," Odysseus continued. "Eggs are one of a boar's favorite treats. And if you will just shut up for a moment,

Mentor, we might even be able to hear him coming."

A hundred objections sprang into Mentor's mind. But he could tell that Odysseus was in no mood for any of them.

Just then Odysseus' eyebrows, like two wings of flame, went up, and his fingers tightened on the shaft of the great spear. "Listen!"

Mentor strained to hear something. Except for the breeze teasing the tops of the bushes, except for the far-away *whit-whit-whit* of a partridge, all he could hear was the dull drumming of his own blood.

And then he, too, heard the sound. It was a brutish commotion, as if some bulky creature was forcing its way through the bushes, trampling on the scrub; like a long and awful sentence punctuated with grunts.

"How close . . . ?" Mentor managed to get out of his dry mouth.

"Let's find out," Odysseus said.

"Let's not!" Mentor whispered, but it was too late. Odysseus was already crawling forward, already up on one knee, the long spear uplifted in his right hand. His left hand pointed toward the east.

Carefully Mentor poked his head up through the bushes.

The boar—black as a cave's mouth—was a good bow shot away, ripping up bushes with its enormous tusks.

Suddenly, hiding in the bushes didn't seem like such a good idea.

Mentor hissed to Odysseus, "It's as big as a mule."

"Bigger!" Odysseus smiled, then for a moment looked over his shoulder. "What's wrong with you, Mentor? We've been on hunts before."

"Hares," Mentor said frantically. "Wild sheep. Deer. Nothing with tusks!" Mentor could feel his voice rise. "And this boar has already killed three men, has made orphans of nine children."

"Then our glory will be all the greater when we slay it," said Odysseus. His eyes were enormous.

CHAPTER TWO

FIRST BLOOD

e need to get the boar's attention," Odysseus said.

"No, we don't."

Odysseus ignored him. "So this is what I want you to do."

Mentor's mouth went even drier, if that was possible. "Me?"

"Just stand up and wave your arms. Till the boar sees you."

"Me?" Now his mouth felt like it was stuffed with Egyptian cotton.

"Stop worrying," Odysseus said. "Boars have notoriously bad eyesight."

"I'm sure that's a great comfort."

Odysseus sighed and shifted his weight. He put his left hand around his right wrist to help hold the weight of the spear. "Really—there's nothing to worry about, Mentor."

"I hate it when you say that."

The big black boar had trotted over to another patch of brush and was now ripping it up and grunting with pleasure.

"Look," Odysseus whispered, "I'll be hidden right here in front of you. As soon as the boar comes close, I'll jump up and spear him. Just like my father did when he and the other heroes slew the great boar of Calydon."

"I thought the great boar of Calydon killed or maimed half of the men in the hunt before anyone slew him," Mentor said.

"Do you want to be a hero or not?" asked Odysseus.

"Right now," Mentor said carefully, trying not to let the hand holding the sewing-needle javelin shake too much, "I'm not sure."

Odysseus sighed. "If we go back with no prize to show, we're going to look like fools. Or worse. Like *cowards*!"

"We'll only look like boys, Odysseus. Which we are." Mentor knew the argument was already lost. There was no greater disgrace for an Achaean warrior than to be thought a coward—man or boy. He stood slowly and waved his hands. "This is a really bad idea."

The black boar ignored him and continued rooting in the briars.

Mentor waved his hands more vigorously.

"Don't you feel like a hero now?" Odysseus asked.

"I feel like a fool," Mentor answered flatly. "I just don't want to feel like a *dead* fool. How fast do you suppose that boar can run between its bit of brush and ours?"

"Not so fast that I can't get my spear into it," said Odysseus. He was holding the spear with both hands now. "Shout, Mentor! Let it know you're over here."

"Hoi! Widow maker! Over this way," Mentor cried.

The black boar paused in its egg hunt and looked up. Its small piggy eyes searched out the source of the sound. Swinging its massive head back and forth, it finally focused directly on Mentor.

"Again," Odysseus whispered. "You've got his attention now."

Mentor's lips felt more padded than his leggings. He couldn't make another sound. The boar was now heading toward their thicket at a lope.

"Is it coming?" Odysseus whispered.

All Mentor could manage was a grunt, much like the boar's.

Slowly Odysseus stood, peering over the bush. He could feel the boar's hooves drumming on the earth. Then he saw it.

"What a monster!" he cried appreciatively.

Behind him Mentor was silent.

"I'm ready," Odysseus cried. "Hold your ground, Mentor. Keep him coming."

"I don't . . ." Mentor managed to croak, "don't think I could stop it if I tried."

The boar was now only a few yards away. Its tusks seemed gigantic and sharp and curved and deadly.

Finally upright, Odysseus braced the long spear against his body, the bronze point aimed at the boar's heart.

The boar lowered its head for the attack, grunted twice, and then plowed into the brush.

Bronze spearhead met bristly hide right above the breastbone, lodging there for a moment before the wooden spear shaft snapped in two. The broken stump of the weapon dropped from Odysseus' numbed hands.

"Oooof!" he grunted.

Mentor shrieked, "Odysseus, no!"

Odysseus twisted away from the boar's continuing charge, but a second too late. One of the tusks scored a ragged gash down his right thigh. Like lightning, pain flashed along his leg. He fell back against Mentor, biting back a scream.

The boar ran on past them, further into the brush.

"Odysseus—are you alive?" Mentor cried.

"Get . . . your . . . javelin." Odysseus' face was screwed in pain.

Only then did Mentor realize that he had dropped

the thing. He bent to pick it up and when he stood again, he saw that the boar had broken through the other side of the thicket and was making a large circle back toward them, snorting with rage.

"One . . . good . . . throw . . ." said Odysseus, carefully speaking through his pain. "That's . . . all . . . you . . . need."

Mentor licked his dry lips and hefted the javelin in his right hand. He had thrown in competition with other boys, had hunted small game, but how could he hope to stop this great beast with what was really no more than a toy?

"Look . . . in . . . eye . . ." Odysseus said.

Mentor could hardly breathe. He kept his own eye fixed on the boar. His heart seemed to be pounding in time with the boar's hoofbeats.

And then—as the beast came within striking range—Mentor felt his own breath stop. His arm seemed to drive forward by itself, sending the javelin flying. The javelin wobbled a bit in its flight, and the sound it made was a strange *whoosh*.

Then everything went dark.

Eyes closed, Mentor waited for the boar to rip him to shreds.

"You . . . did . . . it!" Odysseus was hitting him on the leg.

Mentor opened his eyes. The boar was speeding away from them, the javelin trailing from its flank.

"But I didn't *kill* it," Mentor said miserably. "All I did was make it madder." He paused. "And lost us our only weapon."

"Real . . . weapon . . . here," said Odysseus, touching a finger to his head. "Help . . . me . . . up!"

"You can't run on that leg," Mentor said.

"Not . . . run," Odysseus told him. "Roll." He pointed behind them to the steep slope.

Glancing nervously over at the boar, which had now managed to shake the small javelin loose, Mentor whispered, "Are you crazy, Odysseus? That slope's a hundred feet down if it's a—"

"Take . . . hold." Without waiting for an answer, Odysseus grabbed Mentor's arm and hauled himself to his feet.

Mentor wheeled Odysseus around, and they headed back the way they had come. They plowed through the tangled thicket toward the edge of the slope while the boar was still making up its mind whether to charge again. Mentor half carried, half dragged Odysseus, who hobbled as best he could.

"Faster . . ." Odysseus said, gasping with pain.

Behind them they could hear the boar bellowing as it started to charge again.

"Faster . . ."

"I'm going as fast as I can," Mentor said through clenched teeth.

"Talking . . . to . . . myself," Odysseus said. "Not . . .

you." He took a deep breath and said in a rush, "Better leave me. Only slowing you down."

"Heroes together or not at all," Mentor told him, and just then they reached the edge of the slope.

Slipping free of Mentor's grasp, Odysseus pitched himself forward, going head over heels. Mentor slid after on his bottom, thinking that there was no hope for his tunic now.

Thorns and shards of flint tore at their clothing and flesh. Every bump and knock jarred their bodies, till Mentor began to think they would have had an easier time with the boar.

Then they landed in a heap at the bottom, fetching up against a spindly tree.

"Odysseus, are you . . . ?"

"Keep . . . still," Odysseus said.

Mentor raised his eyes warily and saw the boar standing at the top of the slope, stamping the grass in frustration. He opened his mouth to speak.

"Remember . . . poor . . . eyesight," Odysseus said. "Small brain."

Mentor shut his mouth.

Time seemed to drag by as the boar shook its massive head and peered down the slope. But at last, seeing nothing and hearing nothing, it gave one last grunt and snort, and disappeared back to the bushes to finish its breakfast.

When the boar didn't return, Mentor whispered, "We

need to get you back down to your grandfather's palace so your wound can be properly tended, Odysseus. But meanwhile . . ." He stripped off his linen leggings and, using them as a makeshift bandage, bound up the gaping wound on Odysseus' leg.

"Thanks," Odysseus said. His normally ruddy face was blanched with pain.

"Being a hero," Mentor said, "is awfully bloody work."

"Isn't . . . it . . ." Odysseus said, and then, unaccountably, he grinned.

CHAPTER THREE

THE OLD THIEF

"**H**old still, Master Odysseus," his mother's old nurse, Menaera, snapped impatiently as she bathed his leg with cold water. "The wind may make the tree's branches tremble, but it cannot heal the broken limb."

"That stings!" Odysseus cried.

Drying his leg roughly with a coarse towel, Menaera showed him no mercy. "Not even bad enough to call in the physician, my princeling." She examined the wound closely, sniffing at it for contagion and finding none.

"You're worse than that boar," he complained.

A smile spread over Menaera's wrinkled face. "Now, now! You sound like a child, not a hero. First the bile and then the honey, little man." She spread a pale yellow paste over his wound.

"Ouch! Ouch!" he cried again, which was only half of what he really wanted to say. The paste smarted like vinegar on an open sore. He tried to yank his leg away, but Menaera seized his ankle with a strength that a Cyclops would have envied.

"Ooof. Let me go, old lady."

"A lady, am I?" Menaera laughed.

All the while Mentor sat on a seat in a corner of the room, smirking.

The pungent smell of the yellow paste made Odysseus' eyes water, and he turned his head away, afraid the old woman or Mentor would think he was crying.

"There, there," Menaera soothed. "Where there's stink, there's cure."

"Then," Odysseus said, "I'm entirely cured."

Mentor laughed, clapping his hands.

"Never you mind, young man," Menaera said, turning to Mentor. "I'll fix all your little scratches next. We'll see if you bear it as well as my young princeling." She began winding a clean bandage around Odysseus' thigh.

"Hah!" Odysseus said. Then, "Ow! Menaera—that's too tight."

"Keep still, boy. The stag cries where the doe stands quiet. I swear you are twice the trouble your mother was when she was half your age." She kept winding.

"I'm an Achaean warrior," Odysseus said, puffing out

his chest. "The gods expect me to make trouble."

"For your enemies, perhaps," Menaera said, coming to the end of the bandage. "But not for your old nurse."

Odysseus made a sour face. "I don't have any enemies."

Menaera laughed. "Give it time, my little olive." So saying, she gave the bandage a final yank.

"Owowowow!"

Mentor collapsed with laughter. When he recovered, he said, "She looks after you well."

"I'd rather be lashed by the Furies than be so well attended." Odysseus gritted his teeth while Menaera tied up the bandage.

Pursing her thin lips, Menaera regarded her work with a nod of satisfaction. "Now rest that leg until the wound has closed. A pot half-baked will surely break." She winked at Mentor over Odysseus' head. "No man ever won the gods' favor without a little pain. Your turn, Master Mentor."

Mentor bore the old nurse's ministrations better than Odysseus, but of course his wounds were less severe. He merely ground his teeth till he was afraid he would break them off.

When Menaera finally gathered up her bowls of balms and the linen bandages and left, both Odysseus and Mentor let out deep sighs of relief.

"She's never short of an adage, that one," Mentor

commented. He looked rather spotty, for Menaera had daubed every scratched and torn place with a whitish paste.

Odysseus grunted. "Old women think everything they say is wise just because they're old."

"And young men think everything they do is brave just because it's dangerous," came a deep voice from the doorway.

"Grandfather!" Odysseus cried out. He tried to stand to greet the old robber prince, but his leg gave way and he fell back onto the bench. "I . . . I am a prince of sea-girt Ithaca, Grandfather. I can't very well *shrink* from danger."

Grandfather Autolycus stood with both hands on the doorjambs, frowning in disapproval. "Right this moment I have swineherds who look more princely than you do."

"Sir, we haven't had time to bathe . . ." Mentor said, his normally pale face flushed beneath the white spots.

This time Odysseus stood, though most of the weight was on his left leg. "There's nothing dishonorable, sir, in the scars of battle. You have shown me yours and never apologized for them." He ran a hand through his unruly hair and found it matted with dirt. "It's not my fault that the spear broke at a vital moment."

"Before you steal something," Autolycus said, "be certain it's worth the stealing! *That's* the first rule of successful thievery."

"I didn't know thieves had rules." The pain in Odysseus' leg was like fire, but he swore to himself that he wouldn't show that it hurt.

"Hermes is most particular about the rules of his craft," Autolycus said. "Corollary to rule one: if a spear's on the wall gathering dust, chances are it's not worth much." He came into the room, wrinkling his nose at the smell of the medicines.

"But only yesterday you said how much that spear meant to you." Odysseus sat down again.

"Sentimental value puts no coin in your purse," Autolycus replied. "And it will *not* bring down a boar."

The vertical line appeared between Odysseus' eyes, signaling he was about to lie. Only Mentor noticed.

Odysseus leaned forward. "Owl-eyed Athena appeared to me in a dream," he said. "In her hand was a spear just like the one in your trophy room. When I woke, I knew that the goddess wanted me to take the spear of my illustrious grandfather and hunt a man-killing boar as had my illustrious father."

Autolycus made a strange sound, half laugh, half snort. "And did things go as the goddess intended?"

"Well, some rival god—Pan maybe—or . . . or . . ."

"Ares?" put in Mentor.

"Yes!" Odysseus said. "Or Ares broke the spear. Afraid that a mere mortal would outshine them in glory."

Autolycus could not hold back his laughter. He howled, and all Odysseus could do was look down at the floor and outlast the gale.

Finally Autolycus said, "Oh, grandson, you wriggle like a serpent to escape the trap of your own folly. You amuse me. You really do! Don't put on the gods what are your own faults."

Odysseus said nothing.

"If you'd taken a closer look at your stolen spear," Autolycus continued, "you'd have seen a crack running through the shaft. Which is why I stopped using it."

"It was dark, sir," said Mentor, trying to help his friend out.

"Ah, the wise counselor." Autolycus turned toward Mentor and glared at him. "The hero's friend. And where were you all this time?"

"By his side, sir." Mentor's voice broke under the old man's stare.

"You should have been talking him out of such foolishness."

Mentor chewed his lip. Should he tell Autolycus the complete truth—how he'd been dragged unwilling from his bed and had argued with Odysseus each step of the way? That would only make Odysseus look worse in his grandfather's eyes.

"It seemed a good idea at the time, sir," he mumbled. "The hunt, the glory . . ."

"Ah yes," Autolycus said. "Glory. A poorer provider than sentiment."

"An old man's answer," mumbled Odysseus, but low

enough so that his grandfather could ignore it if he so chose.

Just then a servant appeared in the doorway, holding out a spear to his master. "The men are prepared, my lord, and the dogs ready."

Autolycus took the spear and, for all his years, hefted it as if it were a twig. "I'll be right there." He waved the servant away. "Now *this* is a proper spear. If you'd managed to steal this," he said to Odysseus, "it would have been a deed worthy of respect."

"There's still time for that," Odysseus said defiantly.

"Not on that leg, I fear," Autolycus said. He turned to leave, saying over his shoulder, "I'll bring the boar back, and you can feast upon him in revenge for the ill done you." Then he was gone.

Odysseus spat in disgust. "A bitter feast that will be."

CHAPTER FOUR

A HERO'S TALE

he hunters came back from the hunt with the boar and—from what Mentor could find out—only one dog lost to its tusks.

"So we're invited to the feast tonight."

"I'm not going." Odysseus crossed his arms and lay back on his pallet. "Tell them the wound is too painful. Say I'm asleep."

But Autolycus himself came to escort the boys. "You can walk, or I can have you brought in a litter," he told his grandson.

"I'll walk," Odysseus said sullenly. *Nothing* would have induced him to be carried in. But he used a stick because putting too much weight on the leg made the pain unbearable.

In the feast room Autolycus, splendid in his purple robe, sat in a carved ebony chair. Behind him was a bright fresco of wild cattle being caught and tamed.

Odysseus reclined on a couch on his grandfather's right while Mentor perched on a stool next to Odysseus. The heroes of the hunt and other men of Parnassus filled the rest of the chairs and couches, chattering and joking about the day's events.

At the three-legged cauldron, a slave stirred an ox stew. The smoke drifted up through the opening in the roof, obscuring for a moment the night blue of the sky.

"Smells good," whispered Mentor, his face bright red, having been scrubbed clean of the white paste.

Odysseus said nothing.

"Better than your sickroom and old Menaera's balms."

Still Odysseus was silent.

"Well, you can sulk if you want," Mentor said. "But as for me—I'm famished!" He rose and went to one of the long wooden tables where baskets of flat loaves of bread and bowls full of pomegranates, olives, and figs had been set out.

As if the entire company had the same idea at the same time, the room erupted into a frenzy of eating. Whole kraters of wine were soon emptied and new jars brought in.

Suddenly Autolycus banged his knife on the rim of

his gold cup, a clear signal for silence. "Let us hear the bard now. Shall he tell us a tale of the Argonauts?"

The room burst into a riot of sound. *"Argo! Argo! Argo!"*

Mentor sang out with the rest of them.

Only Odysseus, still nursing his anger, was silent.

The singer was a man called Phonos, who had an amazingly stiff black beard and sun-bronzed skin. He was blind, his eyes as round and black as ripe olives. A slave girl led him to the very center of the room, where he stood by the central hearth.

"My lord, sirs, young gentlemen," Phonos said, "I will sing of the *Argo* and the mighty heroes who sailed on her."

He placed his hands on his hips, threw his head back, and began:

> *"The heaven-sent wind filled the swelling sail*
> *And the swift-oared ship shot through the Clashing Rocks*
> *Like a feathered arrow from a huntsman's bow.*
> *The angry stones scraped the painted stern*
> *Like a wolf snapping at the tail of a hare,*
> *And then Jason's brave crew were safe*
> *Upon the bosom of the wine-dark sea. . . ."*

Apart from the bard's deep, lilting voice, a complete silence fell over the feasting hall. The singer held all eyes, all ears, till the very end of the tale.

And then the hall erupted once more, this time with loud applause and cheers. Even Odysseus had been caught up in the story, and he applauded with the rest.

Autolycus rose and presented the singer with a brooch of silver. "Small recompense for your splendid tale," he said.

At his grandfather's words, the spell of the story was broken. Once again Odysseus felt the twin throbbing of his wound and his shame. He snatched up his cup and drained it. The watered wine helped dull the pain in his leg but did nothing for the pain in his heart.

"Wasn't that exciting?" Mentor whispered.

Wiping the thin line of wine from his upper lip, Odysseus said, "One day my adventures will draw cheers like that."

"I'm still smarting from *your* adventures," Mentor told him. "Can't you just enjoy the feast?"

Odysseus turned to his friend. "Don't you see, Mentor? *We* should have brought home the boar. *We* should have been toasted at the feast."

"*We* are lucky to be alive," Mentor said sensibly.

"Alive without glory," Odysseus snapped, "is not alive at all."

"Your father wouldn't say so," Mentor told him. "He specifically asked me to keep an eye on you."

"*My* father sailed on the *Argo*," Odysseus said. "*He* faced countless dangers and returned with the Golden

Fleece. And"—his face was a misery—"no one was assigned to nursemaid *him*."

"I'm no nursemaid!"

As if he hadn't heard Mentor at all, Odysseus continued, "And how far have I traveled from my rocky little island? No farther than to my grandfather's home."

Mentor came and knelt by the couch. "Those heroic days are over, Odysseus. The Argonauts are home. There's peace everywhere. The treasures are all found, the monsters all slain. Be sensible."

"*Sensible?*" Odysseus' anger pulled him upright on the couch. "You can be sensible, my friend. But I know there are still adventures and monsters aplenty. Only not here in Parnassus. And not in *Ithaca*!" His face had turned bright red.

Mentor held out his plate. There was a bit of bread left, a few olives, black and round as the bard's eyes. "Here. Eat something. Hunger is a monster easily conquered."

"You sound like Menaera," Odysseus said, but he ate.

Suddenly the door opened, and a priest walked across the feast hall holding a pair of huge tusks. Behind him came a boy carrying a silver plate on which sat the boar's tongue.

The priest laid the tusks at Autolycus' feet.

Odysseus knew those tusks all too well. Intimately in fact. His wound throbbed in recognition.

Picking up the tusks, Autolycus stood and declared, "Men of Parnassus, the beast that terrorized our countryside has this day been slain. Courage and skill have brought us this victory!"

A great cheer went up, and wine cups clashed together.

Then Autolycus plucked the boar's tongue from the silver plate and walked over to the hearth. Flinging the meat into the fire, he said, "I offer this share of the kill to the gods."

The tongue sizzled on the flame, and the sweet, thick smell of it went straight up toward the hole in the roof.

"To Apollo whose light guided us, to Artemis who led us to the prey, to Ares who gave us strength for the fight. The rest is for us."

A round of good-natured laughter followed, and—right on cue—servants entered the room bearing plates of roasted boar.

Even as those were passed around, Autolycus called for silence once more.

"Those who were with me today know the truth of our hunt. But I tell it now for all to hear. When we came upon the boar, that mighty man killer, widow maker, who made orphans of nine children in ten days, he was already sorely used. His wind was gone. His legs had no speed left in them. His fury had been blunted by fatigue." He looked around the room as he spoke.

"Yes!" called one of the hunters. "He was a broken reed already."

"Hardly worth the climb!" shouted another.

"We took this as a gift from the Fates," Autolycus continued. "But when we field-dressed the beast, preparing to take him down the mountain, we found this embedded in his heart." He raised his hand and held up something for the company to see. There was a long fragment of bronze glinting between his fingers.

Mentor hit Odysseus on the shoulder with his fist. "Look! Look!"

"My spear point," Odysseus whispered. "It must have broken off in the boar."

"This bronze had already taken half the beast's life," Autolycus declared, turning toward Odysseus. "The glory of the hunt therefore belongs not just to me and my hunters, but to my grandson, Odysseus, who struck this first deadly blow and took a grievous blow himself in return."

All eyes turned to the boy on the couch. His name was suddenly on everyone's lips.

"Odysseus!" they cried. "Young prince of Ithaca!"

Odysseus picked up the walking stick and, trembling, stood. He ran his fingers through his hair, then acknowledged the cheers with a slight bob of his head.

"Tell us the tale, Odysseus," someone cried.

"How did you do it?" called another.

His grandfather nodded. "The story, my boy," he said, smiling.

For a moment Odysseus felt nervous. He cleared his

throat, lifted his chin. *I'll give them a tale,* he thought, *that they'll remember for years.* He recalled how the bard had stood, and thrust the stick away. It fell back against the couch. He put his hands on his hips and—never minding the pain in his leg—began the way he'd been taught:

> "*Apollo's chariots had scarce cleared the flank*
>   *Of Parnassus' rugged heights—*"

"Louder!" someone called.
He made an effort to raise his voice.

> "*When bold Odysseus' eagle eye spied out the trail.*
>   *Spear in hand, he stalked the fearsome beast.*
>   *And then it came—charging through the grass*
>   *Like . . . er . . . er . . . a storm that drives over the sea.*
>   *With his grandsire's sturdy spear*
>   *Held firmly in his grasp,*
>   *He met the fierce attack, unyielding,*
>   *Like the rock that er . . . er . . . breaks a crashing wave.*"

"Go on, young prince," came a cry, which momentarily broke his concentration, but he took another deep breath and went on.

> "*The tusks of the boar gouged deep*
>   *A dreadful wound on the hunter's leg.*
>   *But as it left him there for dead*
>   *It carried its own doom in its heart.*"

There was an enormous roar of approval as he finished. But when Odysseus looked over to where Mentor was sitting, his friend had turned his face away.

Odysseus felt a stab of pain in his thigh, as though he'd been wounded a second time. Turning back to the listeners, he raised his hand for silence. "There is a little more," he said.

The men were silent, waiting, and Odysseus began again.

> "But brave Odysseus would not have lived
>   To tell of his matchless deed
>   Had not the faithful Mentor,
>   Friend from boyhood, wise Mentor,
>   Stood over the injured warrior,
>   As a shepherd over a smitten ram
>   From the teeth of a ravenous wolf,
>   Even at the risk of his own life."

He did not dare turn again to look at Mentor, but suddenly Mentor's name was on everyone's lips.

"And there is yet a bit more," Odysseus called out.

> "As unflinching as Parnassus itself,
>   In the face of the north wind's fury,
>   Mentor raised his spear and threw it."

From behind him he heard Mentor whisper, "Javelin,

not spear." But *javelin* did not have the force in the verse, so Odysseus ignored truth for story and continued.

> *"He struck the beast a second wound*
> *And put the widow maker to flight."*

He ended the story by letting his head drop slightly, as the bard had done.

The applause and cheers for his story made him feel good. But even better was the grin on Mentor's face.

His grandfather, too, was smiling. So daringly, Odysseus called out, "Grandfather, what trophy of this hunt can I take back to Ithaca?"

Autolycus roared with laughter. "Oh, you are my grandson indeed!" he said. "Well . . ." He pursed his lips. "The tusks will stay here on Parnassus where they were won. They shall be carved into scales for my helmet. But this"—he pressed the broken spearhead into Odysseus' palm—"will be your trophy. I'll have my metalsmith drill a hole in it so it can hang by a leather cord around your neck. Let it be a reminder of both your courage and your folly."

Odysseus smiled. "Grandfather, where there's victory, there's no folly."

Who, thought Mentor, *sounds like the old woman now!*

CHAPTER FIVE

DANGEROUS VOYAGE

 month later, Autolycus drove the boys down the coast himself, in a chariot pulled by two large, sturdy horses.

"There!" he cried above the noise of the chariot wheels, the snorting of the horses, and the bellowing of a gusty wind. "The ship to take you home."

Odysseus looked over to the sandy harbor where the ship was beached. Sailors swarmed over the open deck and tested the mast, the oars.

"Is it big enough, Grandfather?" Odysseus sounded skeptical. "There seem to be only seven oars on each side." He had arrived in a much larger ship.

"Big enough to carry the two of you and the gifts I am sending home with you," Autolycus said. He urged the horses ahead with a slap of the reins. "By way of compensation for the injury you suffered under my care."

Without thinking, Odysseus touched his right leg. The wound was well healed. All that was left was a bright-red scar that Menaera promised would fade after a while, though Odysseus hoped it would not fade altogether.

Mentor laughed. "His father grows rich on Odysseus' folly."

Autolycus laughed with him. "Just as well my grandson didn't lose a leg, or I would have been left a pauper."

Reining in the horses, Autolycus gave the care of the chariot to a nearby slave. Then turning to the boys, he said, "Come, see all that goes with you."

By then a cart had come to a halt next to them. The boys watched as three men began the task of unloading the gifts. A pair of bronze tripods, several painted clay bowls, a polished sword, a massive two-handed gold goblet, a casket of jewels, a footstool inlaid with ebony, and a fir-wood box carved with pictures of lions and gryphons. They were all taken onto the ship.

"That box looks familiar," Odysseus said.

"So it should," said Autolycus with a smirk. "I stole it from your father the last time I visited his palace."

"Grandfather!" Odysseus said in mock horror. "Stealing from your son-in-law?"

Autolycus grinned. "Just keeping my hand in. He'll be glad to see it back. If indeed he ever noticed it was gone. And your mother will be pleased with what I am sending her, too: those agate beads she loves so well, and three bronze finger rings. And another ring of white onyx. And Hera only knows what else. Woman stuff. Menaera picked them out for me." He wrinkled his nose. "And I have something special for Mentor as a parting gift."

"For me?" Mentor's voice rose to an alarming squeak.

"For the young hero who saved my grandson. Here." He handed Mentor a golden signet ring. "Do you see the carving?"

Mentor held the ring up so that the sun glinted on it. "A boar hunt!" he said.

"And finished by my goldsmith just this morning, or I would have given it to you before," Autolycus said.

"Sir, I'm overwhelmed . . ." Mentor began.

"Quick, put it on your finger," Odysseus said, his arm around his friend's shoulder, "or he'll have it back from you and hidden away before you know it."

They walked down toward the ship, a black-tarred beauty with a red-and-white eye painted on its side. Mentor trailed slightly behind, admiring his new ring.

"What was in the box when you took it?" Odysseus asked. "In case Father is angry."

Autolycus shook his head. "It was empty when I stole it, worse luck. So I'm sending it back just as empty. I may be a thief, but at least I'm an honest one."

Mentor had caught up by then and heard the last sentence.

They all three laughed at that, Autolycus loudest of all.

At the sound of their laughter, the burly captain of the ship started toward them.

"It's a fine ship, and a good crew," he called out. "You'll be proud, my king."

Autolycus went to meet him. "Tros, you old pirate." They grasped hands and began speaking rapidly, one to the other.

"That ship would look better to me," Odysseus said quietly to Mentor, "if it weren't taking us back home."

Mentor refused to be discouraged. He grasped his friend's shoulder. "But it'll be a *real* voyage this time, Odysseus. We'll be going the whole length of the Great Gulf—not just taking the short crossing to Ithaca."

Autolycus and the captain had finished their conversation and joined the boys.

"Real voyage, eh?" said the captain, his broad face wreathed by a scraggly beard. There was a slashing scar down from his right eyebrow to his chin. "By sea is quicker. Safer, too. You never know what sort of robbers you might run into by the road. Begging your pardon, Autolycus, but you're—"

"A thief, not a robber." Autolycus clapped the captain on the back to show he held no hard feelings. "A fine distinction from a seaman who has done some pirating of his own!"

"The sea has its own dangers," Odysseus mused.

Mentor noted that he sounded more hopeful than scared.

"A few," Tros agreed, fingering the scar on his cheek. "But we know how to handle them."

"My soothsayer consulted the oracles not once but twice for this trip," Autolycus said. "He assures me that you'll have good weather, calm seas, and a fruitful voyage. And I'll hold Captain Tros responsible if you don't."

"Hold the gods responsible for the seas, not me!" Tros retorted. "I assure you we'll take proper care of your young princeling."

"You will indeed—or have me to answer to!" Autolycus warned.

Odysseus made a face.

"Try not to be too disappointed, grandson," said Autolycus.

Two days later, as Mentor bent over the side of the ship, the last of his breakfast disappearing into the white-capped waves, Odysseus laughed. "So much for Grandfather's soothsayer."

Mentor groaned in response. "I've nothing left in my belly."

Black clouds scudded across the sky. Cold winds from the north blown by the god Boreas filled the sail, but the water had turned a dark, forbidding green. Riding high on the waves, the little ship lurched alarmingly.

"Of course," Odysseus continued, "soothsayers only tell people what they want to hear; otherwise who'd pay them?"

Mentor moaned again. He was wrong. There was still some bit of breakfast left, and it, too, was threatening a return.

Odysseus patted him on the back. "As I remember, you were the one looking forward to this voyage."

Mentor's groan had turned to a constant low moaning.

"Try to enjoy it."

Odysseus left Mentor to his complaints and found Captain Tros standing with one hand braced against the mast. The sail had long since been hauled down and stowed away, safe from the storm, and the oarsmen strained at their work. The broad-bladed oars knifed into the water in powerful, rhythmic strokes.

"How bad is it really?" Odysseus asked.

Tros looked up into the wind, squinting. "Hard to tell. We could turn back and beach her till the storm passes. On the other hand, we're only a day's sail from Ithaca, and we could head there. But that would mean going into the teeth of this wind."

He saw the alarm in Odysseus' eyes and misread it. "All will be fine, Prince Odysseus, trust me. She's a sturdy ship."

"I'm not afraid," said Odysseus. He did not add that his alarm was at ending the voyage too soon in Ithaca, where his mother and father would fuss over him and keep him from any more adventures. *Till I am an old man,* he thought. *As old as Tros here.*

"All the omens were good when we left," Tros said. Then he turned and—more to himself than Odysseus— murmured, "Perhaps we can make harbor at Zacynthus."

For the first time, Odysseus actually smiled and touched a hand to the spearhead amulet around his neck. "The *Argo* came through worse than this."

"That it did, Prince Odysseus," said Tros. Then he turned to shout at the oarsmen. "Put your backs to it, boys! Let me see those muscles rip!"

Odysseus looked for a moment at the straining oars- men, then he returned to where Mentor was emptying his stomach once again, this time of nothing more than bile.

The storm got worse, not better, with waves breaking over the ship and landing each time with the force of a club on bare skin. Tros ordered the oars drawn in since there was little the oarsmen could do in such a tur- bulent sea.

All around Odysseus and Mentor, the men began to pray.

"Poseidon, save us," cried a sailor not much older than Mentor, but well muscled from his time at the oars.

"Triton, hear our prayers," sang out another.

Either the gods weren't listening or they weren't in

the mood to grant wishes. Hour after hour, the ship was driven helplessly beneath an olive-black sky. Each new wave lifted her up, then slammed her down again with an impact that made the planks shudder and the men cry out anew.

"Poseidon!"

"Triton!

"Nereus!"

"Save us!"

Mentor let go of the side of the boat long enough to turn to Odysseus. "This is your fault, you know."

"My fault?"

A wave splashed between them.

"You forgot to give thanks to Athena."

"When?" Odysseus asked. "I always remember Athena. I was dedicated to her as an infant." He started to slip on the wet deck and grabbed on to the railing.

"Well, you forgot this time," Mentor insisted. "Back at the feast. When you were telling everyone what great heroes we were. You should have thanked Athena for guiding our spears. But you didn't."

"It must have . . ." The crease between Odysseus' eyes deepened. "Must have slipped my mind."

"Did it slip your mind that Poseidon's her uncle?" Mentor said, his face now gray, now green, now . . . over the ship's side. He threw up nothing and sank back onto the deck. "The god of the sea."

Odysseus sat down next to him and put a hand on

Mentor's shoulder. "If someone forgot to thank me for something, I wouldn't punish a whole boatload of sailors for it."

"You're ... not ... a ... god," said Mentor and retched again, this time into his own lap. Luckily his stomach was empty.

"Then I'll thank the goddess now." Odysseus stood, both hands gripping the railing.

"Owl-eyed Athena," he called, "forgive this small prince who wanted too much to be a hero."

Mentor grabbed hold of Odysseus' tunic and, pulling himself up to stand by his friend's side, he put one hand on the side of the ship, raising the other to the black sky. "I, too, Athena, ask forgiveness that I didn't remind Odysseus of his duty."

At that very moment, the ship was pitched up into the air by a great wave, as black as the sky, as high as a mountain.

For a second the little boat hovered between sea and sky, between life and death.

Then it dropped.

Still waving, Mentor was flung overboard into the sea.

Odysseus was quick, but not quick enough. His fingers touched the hem of Mentor's tunic for a moment before the boy was gone.

"Mentor!" Odysseus cried. He thought he could make out Mentor's thin figure through a haze of sea spray. "Mentor!" he cried again, his hands gripping so hard on the wooden rail that an imprint was left in his palms.

For a moment he thought about diving after his friend, but he was afraid that he might not be strong enough with his weakened leg.

Just then something smacked him painfully on that very leg. He looked down. It was the fir-wood box his grandfather had given them, come loose of its lashings. He knew it was empty and could see that the lid was sealed with wax to keep the interior dry on the voyage.

Just the thing, he thought.

Seizing the box with both hands, he heaved it over the side of the boat and jumped into the waves after it.

Sure enough, the box bobbed on top of the water. Odysseus kept it in sight and caught up after three hard strokes. Then, holding onto one of its wooden handles, he kicked as hard as he could, his bad leg lagging after the good one, steering the box toward the place where he'd last seen Mentor floundering in the sea.

"Mentor!" he cried, then was sorry he had spoken as a wave dashed into his mouth. It felt like the entire ocean went in, and only a bit got coughed back out.

But Mentor heard the coughing, spotted him, and managed to swim close enough so that Odysseus could maneuver the box between them, a handle on each side.

"Hold on," he called. "We can kick ourselves back to the ship."

"Gone," Mentor managed in a voice made hoarse by the salt water. "Gone."

Odysseus turned and gulped. An immense billow was rising up behind him like a huge, green, cyclopean wall. When the sea had flattened out again, he saw that Mentor was right.

The ship *was* gone.

They were alone in the middle of the heaving sea.

CHAPTER SIX

MISERY AT SEA

They clung desperately to the box, saying little, conserving strength. The storm continued to rain down on them, drops as large as grapes, but could add little more to their misery. They were already as cold and as wet as they were going to get.

At last—mercifully—the storm subsided. But still the boys bobbed helplessly, now under a brilliant canopy of stars.

"Where are we?" Mentor croaked.

Odysseus looked up. Suddenly he couldn't remember any of the stars over them. He and Mentor might as well have been under an alien sky for all that he could name them.

"If only I'd listened more closely to my tutor . . ." he began.

"*If only* is not a phrase for heroes," Mentor retorted hoarsely.

When the rosy dawn appeared at last, all it revealed was an empty, watery plain.

The little box bobbed more gently now on the calm sea.

"Still alive then?" Odysseus called to Mentor. His own voice was hoarse, his thirst enormous. His hands were cramped with hanging on to the handle of the chest.

"Still . . . alive," Mentor answered. "I . . . think."

"Don't think," Odysseus said. "It's a bad habit. Thinking leads to wondering. Wondering leads to needing. Needing leads to . . ."

"Then . . . pray," Mentor croaked.

Odysseus raised his head. "Athena!" he cried through parched lips.

The goddess didn't seem ready to answer any more prayers.

And really, Odysseus thought suddenly, *since her answers are worse than her silences, perhaps I shouldn't ask for more.* But they definitely needed fresh water. And soon. Mentor was in worse shape than he, having been so ill onboard ship. *I shall have to keep a careful eye on him.*

Suddenly Mentor's grip seemed to slacken, and slowly, soundlessly, he slid under the water.

Odysseus grabbed for him, caught a bit of his tunic, hauled him up again. Boosting his friend up onto the chest, Odysseus held him in place.

"Better the burning sun than a watery tomb," he whispered.

Mentor coughed, moaned, lay still.

To keep both their spirits up, Odysseus began to tell stories about his father and the trip on the *Argo*—about the bronze giant Talos, about the Golden Fleece guarded by the dragon. He wasn't sure that Mentor was even listening, but he kept on till he had no more voice.

Again and again, he scanned the horizon for some sign of land or a ship—

A ship!

He blinked three times and looked again to be sure that what he thought he had seen was true.

It was not a cloud, no.

Not the white crest of a wave.

Definitely a ship's sail.

"Mentor, look!" he cried. "We're saved!"

Atop the floating chest, Mentor stirred sluggishly and with great effort lifted his head. His eyelids fluttered open.

"A ship!" Odysseus repeated, and let out a huge, hoarse laugh.

There was no mistaking the square shape of the sail

now, and—soon enough—a black hull was clearly visible as well.

"What kind of ship?" Mentor croaked.

"The kind that floats," Odysseus said. "The kind we need. Come on. Let's get closer."

He kicked and kicked, the exercise bringing warmth back to his cold legs, driving them relentlessly toward the oncoming ship.

"Praise to the gods," Mentor said, his words emerging in an alarming wheeze.

"It was praying to the gods that got us into this fix," muttered Odysseus. "Let's just help ourselves, Mentor." He kicked some more.

Mentor half raised himself up and waved an arm at the ship.

"Over here," he called out.

"You sound like a frog," Odysseus said.

"You *look* like a frog," Mentor countered.

But they both smiled broadly through cracked lips, and Odysseus kept on kicking.

The ship grew closer still, and they could see figures on the deck pointing at them.

Soon enough they were looking at a row of bearded, bronzed faces, and then a rope snaked down the hull past the painted fish on the side, to dangle in the water in front of them.

"You grab the rope, Mentor, and go up first," Odysseus said. "Can you manage?"

Without answering, Mentor snagged the rope and started to shinny up hand over hand.

The rope was given a good shake from above, and Mentor slid back all the way into the water.

"No, you idiots," came a rough voice from above. "Tie the rope to the box first."

Odysseus bristled at the insult, but they were in no position to argue. So he tied the rope to one of the handles with a firm seaman's knot.

Almost at once the bearded men began hauling it up.

His remaining strength giving way, Mentor slipped under the water.

Without stopping to think, Odysseus caught him under the arms with one hand, and with the other grabbed hold of the box's lower handle. Then he held on to both with all his might.

If the sailors above were aware of the extra weight, they ignored it in their eagerness to get their hands on their prize. Soon box and boys were lifted up and over the side of the ship.

Odysseus and Mentor fell to the deck and lay there gasping.

Saved.

CHAPTER SEVEN

A PRINCESS
OF SPARTA

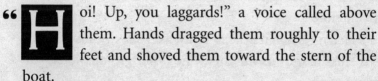oi! Up, you laggards!" a voice called above them. Hands dragged them roughly to their feet and shoved them toward the stern of the boat.

Mentor had not the strength to stay upright, and Odysseus had to support him so that he wouldn't fall forward and smash his face on the deck.

"You look bad enough without flattening your nose," he whispered.

Mentor didn't reply.

At the very rear of the ship two girls were sheltering under a sailcloth awning. The boys were shoved down beside them; then their escort rejoined the rest of the crew in examining the box.

One of the girls, heart-faced, with long, delicate lashes and a cascade of curls, shrank back from them. The other, plainer—as the moon is plainer than the sun—smiled a greeting.

"Helen," she said to her companion, "they are prisoners just as we are. We have nothing to fear from them."

"Fear's not the problem," Helen said, wrinkling her perfect nose and smoothing the folds of her robe. "We don't know where they've come from."

"From the sea actually," Odysseus said, propping Mentor against a large water jar. He took a long drink from the jar and then gave some water to Mentor. "Like a god!" He laughed. "But we don't know where you're from either."

Helen turned her head away, as if she disdained both his speech and his manner. The other girl answered for them both.

"I'm Penelope, daughter of Icarius. This is my cousin Helen."

"*Princess* of Sparta," Helen added tartly, turning back to deliver the line.

The conversation had brought Mentor out of his stupor. He smiled weakly at Helen. "We . . . are—"

Before he could complete his sentence, Odysseus cut him off with a sharp dig in the ribs. *Knowledge is a two-edged weapon, Grandfather Autolycus once said. It can easily be turned upon you.* He didn't want the girls—or this rough-looking crew—to know anything about them until he'd figured out what to do.

"I am Eumeneus," he said. "And this wet frog is my friend Astocles."

"Really," replied Helen, raising a regal eyebrow. "And what family do you come from? Are they important?"

Odysseus thought quickly. He knew that their tunics would give nothing away. Onboard a ship travelers wore the simple garments of sailors, for the salt and sea could ruin good cloth. *Better,* he thought, *to be considered poorer than richer. At least for the moment.* Richer might mean they'd be held for ransom.

"No, not important," he said. "We're swineherds from Cephalonia."

Helen immediately drew back, as if a rat had just scurried between them. But Penelope laughed.

"A swineherd who speaks with a courtier's tongue, Helen."

"My swine are the king's swine, princess. A man with half an ear can learn to how to speak like a man of the court." He grinned, thinking that a good answer.

"Swineherds. Pah!" Helen held her nose as she spoke.

Penelope shook her head. "Since they've just been plucked from the sea," she said sensibly, "they must be clean. Cleaner than we are, certainly."

Turning her back, Helen said sniffily, "A clean swineherd is still only a pig keeper. Hardly fit company for princesses."

Odysseus said nothing, and Mentor sighed and closed his eyes again.

But Penelope turned on her cousin and shook a finger at her. "They're better, surely, than these brutes who abducted us."

"Abducted? How?" Odysseus asked quickly, quietly. He'd been right to keep his rank quiet.

"We were walking along the beach collecting shells," Penelope explained. "Our men were further down the beach, around a bend, collecting firewood, starting a fire. Doing . . . things. As were our maids. Helen was bored and begged me to go with her." She bent toward Odysseus and said in a confiding whisper, "You mustn't mind her. She's been terribly spoiled. Sometimes it's simply easier to go along with her than to fight her."

"I understand, my lady," Odysseus whispered back, one finger against the side of his nose to show his agreement. Then he said, more loudly, "So—shells, beach, alone and . . ."

"And suddenly," Penelope said, her voice matching his, "these brutes appeared from nowhere. From everywhere. We tried to run, but there were too many of them. I almost got away, but then they caught Helen, and she screamed, and I went back for her. I don't know what happened to our men and our maids."

"And just see what they did to me," Helen said. She lifted one of the folds of her tunic to display a tear.

"Father had this imported from Crete especially."

"So they're planning to ransom you," Odysseus said.

The girls looked at one another with anxious eyes.

"Not exactly." Penelope spoke quietly.

Helen leaned forward. "They're planning to sell me to a wealthy king that he may have the most splendid bride in all the world." There was a surprising note of pride in her voice. "They mentioned Theseus, the great king of Athens."

Penelope made a face and turned away.

"Isn't he an old man?" Odysseus asked.

"He's an old *king*," said Helen. "Rich and powerful. But I wouldn't expect a pig boy to understand."

Before Odysseus could answer, a shadow fell across them.

"Get up, you drowned rats," a broad-faced pirate said to Odysseus. "Captain wants to talk to you."

Odysseus helped Mentor to his feet, and they managed to make it across the deck to where the captain was waiting.

The captain reminded Odysseus of a mastiff his father owned. Like the dog, the captain was broad at the shoulder and narrow at the knee, and he carried himself with the same air of watchful aggression. *Be careful of this one,* Odysseus thought, remembering how his father's dog once bit him on the ankle because he'd moved too quickly near the sheep.

"The box," said the captain. "Where did you get it?"

Recalling how quickly Penelope had recognized his fine language, he answered with care. "We be simple swineherds, my lord," Odysseus said, keeping a grip on Mentor's arm.

"Swineherds, eh!" the captain roared. "And were your pigs doing the dog paddle with the fish?" He laughed, and his men were quick to laugh with him.

"We was chasing a sow who run off, great lord," answered Odysseus, being careful not to look right into the captain's eyes. "My mate and me."

Mentor managed a nod of his head.

Odysseus figured the captain believed him now, else he'd have been stopped. So he went on expansively. "Fallen she had, onto a ledge. So we climbed down to get her. Me first. And my mate's foot slipped. I grabbed him by the tunic as he went by. *Whoosh!*" He demonstrated catching Mentor's tunic.

The sailors began to snigger.

"And he pulls me over with him." He windmilled his arms to show how he fell.

The sailors were fully enjoying the tale now.

"And into the water went we," Odysseus finished.

"What about the damned box?" growled the captain. He had, Odysseus noted, teeth like the mastiff's, too.

"Ah, the box," Odysseus said. "It appeared from no-where. A gift of the gods, my lord. Keep it if it please you." He bobbed his head.

The captain let out a short, sharp bark of a laugh and

his men all joined in, like dogs around the leader of the pack.

"It pleases me well," the captain said. "But what should we do about you two pig boys, eh?"

"Let us off at the next habitable stretch of beach?" Odysseus asked. Then, realizing that might be too high-flown an answer, he added, "A dingle, a shingle, a wee bit of sand would make this pig boy's life really grand!" He shuffled his feet in a kind of dance.

Again the captain gave his barking laugh. "Indeed, we already have too many mouths to feed—and not enough room at the oars."

Odysseus nodded his head, trying to show enough gratitude.

"Toss the pig farmers back in the drink," the captain said.

Three men grabbed Odysseus and dragged him to the ship's side. He tried to wrench free, but he hadn't the strength, having spent a night in the water. Besides, they were grown men. *Large* grown men. Large grown men with *muscles*. In a moment, they had him over their heads and were about to toss him overboard.

"Wait!" cried Mentor, coming out of his dazed state. "You're throwing away a king's ransom."

There was a long silence, and Odysseus could see before him only the expanse of sea.

"Bring him here," the captain ordered. "Bring them *both* here."

The world turned end over, and Odysseus found himself with his feet back on the deck again. He'd only an instant to recover before he was face-to-face with the captain once more.

The pirate captain growled at him, sounding exactly like his father's mastiff. "And what makes either of you boys worth a king's ransom?" he said. "You look like pig herders to me."

"You're wrong," Mentor said, his voice desperate. "King Laertes will pay handsomely for the safe return of his son."

Odysseus knew that pirates were merchants—of a sort. Just like his grandfather. *Before you steal something, be certain it's worth the stealing!* A prince would be worth keeping, but there was no profit in feeding and tending his companion. However, if Mentor were thrown back into the sea now, Odysseus knew he'd sink like a stone.

I can't let that happen.

"You're right, Prince Odysseus," he said, turning to Mentor. "And if these men were to harm you, your father would surely not rest till he had his revenge. Not even if he had to set after them aboard the *Argo* herself."

"Odysseus—what are you talking about?" Mentor asked woozily. "You know you're the prince, not I."

"He's been so long in the water, his wits are water-logged," Odysseus said, tipping the captain a sly wink. "Tell me—would a prince wear a cheap scrap of metal like this around his neck?" He pulled the fragment of bronze spearhead from beneath his tunic.

"Not any prince I know," said the captain. Then he looked Mentor over with a practiced eye and, spotting the gold signet ring, he laughed. "Ah, Prince Odysseus, I shall have you—and the ring off your hand." He turned to his men. "You, Phynos and Tsountas, get rid of this one with the red hair. He's too crafty for my liking, and see that scar? He's crippled as well."

Mentor cried out. "No . . ."

Odysseus gave him a mighty shove. "Don't plead for my worthless life, sir. I willingly return to the bosom of Poseidon, knowing you're safe."

He rushed to the side of the ship and threw himself over before his deception could be uncovered, flying for the moment through the air like some ungainly bird.

Then he hit the water with a loud splash.

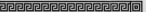

CHAPTER EIGHT

THE THREAD
OF LIFE

n the brief time he'd been aboard the pirate vessel, Odysseus had spotted the one thing that had given him some hope. There had been a flock of seagulls barely visible in the distance.

Where there are gulls, he thought, *there must be land.*

If he could only make it to land, anything was possible.

A fresh ship.

A sword.

Men to follow him.

He worried about Mentor on the ship more than he did about himself in the sea. It was only a matter of time before Mentor's unthinking honesty betrayed him. As soon as the pirates discovered the truth, they'd fling

Mentor over the side of the boat along with their slops.

But only if they were feeling particularly forgiving.

Odysseus swam slowly toward the spot where he'd seen the gulls.

Better thinking than sinking, he told himself. Gritting his teeth, he began swimming with renewed vigor. Both their lives depended upon him reaching land.

Odysseus was actually a strong swimmer when he didn't have high waves, a weakened leg, and a sick friend to contend with. He'd grown up on an island, learning to swim before he could run. He knew not to rely on one kind of stroke, but to rotate several—an overhand for a few minutes, then a more restful sidestroke, then the overhand again, and finally turning on his back, letting his legs do most of the work.

The last time on his back, he not only saw gulls but could hear them as well.

He flipped over and, lifting his head, tried to catch a glimpse of a shore.

There was a smudge on the horizon that might be an island.

He forced himself onward, stopping every hundred strokes or so to tread water. But lack of food, lack of fresh water, and, most of all, lack of sleep were telling on him. His limbs were growing weaker. He had a persistent headache from the sun and the salt. Each time his arm ploughed through the water, it took a greater and greater effort to raise it again. His legs protested, too, especially the right leg. His chest burned as if an iron spike had been driven through it. But still he swam on, now counting the strokes as he went.

One hundred . . . two hundred . . . three hundred . . .

This time the cries of the gulls, which he had taken for encouragement, sounded mocking, as if they were calling out, "Foolish mortal! Neither fish nor fowl."

Water kept splashing into his mouth, though he tried to keep it closed. The salt stung his eyes. His lungs ached with the effort of breathing.

One thousand . . . one hundred . . .

He treaded water again, tried to see if the shore was any closer. But his eyes were cloudy, and he couldn't see a thing.

He was done.

He knew he was done.

Best surrender with grace, he thought.

The sea sucked him down, and he had time for only a single cry.

Then the water was over his head. First blue. Then green. Then gold—shards of it, like coins sparkling over his head.

He'd seen those coins before, when he was a baby, pitched headlong into the calm water of the Bay of Phocis, his first swimming lesson.

No, not coins. He realized that now. A golden thread

above him, where sun met sea. Like the thread of life woven by the three sisters, the Fates. It was Clotho who spun the thread, Lachesis who wove it into the fabric of the world. Finally it was grim Atropos who—at the end of a man's life—cut the thread with her knife.

But I'm not a man yet, he wanted to cry out, as if that had ever made any difference to the Fates. As if one could make a sound beneath the water.

A sound.

Like a chittering.

A whistle.

Recalling the sound of a shepherd directing his flock on land.

Life.

And then something surged below him, stopping his descent: a giant hand beneath him; giant fingers cupping him, lifting him up, pushing hard against the wall of water.

Poseidon? he thought wearily. *Is it you, mighty god of the sea, uncle to my own Athena?* He was too tired to think more.

Looking down for an instant, he thought he saw a pair of Nereids, those beautiful, long-haired sea nymphs that sailors desire. One of them swimming on each side of him, their graceful bodies arcing effortlessly though the water.

And then his head broke through the waves, and he gasped and gasped for air, his eyes dazzled by the light.

The sun blazed like a beacon above him, and his ears were filled with thunder.

The thunder of breakers crashing on the shore.

A final heave of the water threw him forward, and he was suddenly knee-down in shallow water, waves frothing angrily around him. Belching out a stomach full of brine, he crawled painfully up onto the dry beach.

A dingle, a shingle, a wee bit of sand.

For a long while he lay on his side, sucking in air and thinking, *The Nereids. I will honor them. I will make sacrifices to them. I will tell my children and my grandchildren how they saved me.*

Then rolling over onto his stomach and pushing himself up onto his elbows, he stared out at the sea for some sign of his rescuers.

And then he saw them—two fins coursing through the waves side by side.

"Dolphins!" he cried, his voice as torn and ragged as a cloth on a nail. If he hadn't been so exhausted, he would have laughed.

He looked behind him at the land. A rocky height dotted with moss and scrub rose up like a castle wall.

"Must . . . climb," he croaked. "Must . . . find . . . water."

But he could do neither. His thread of life, so nearly cut, could carry him no further. With a groan, he fell back down on the sand and surrendered to the darkness.

CHAPTER NINE

SILENUS

I t was the stink that woke him.

It smelled worse than the dunghills in the courtyards of his father's palace. Worse than the goat pens at the height of summer, when even the flies couldn't stand the smell.

Opening his eyes, Odysseus found himself in the dim interior of a cave. He was lying on a pile of leaves on a packed earth floor with a shaft of sunlight filtering through the cave mouth.

How did I get here? he wondered. *And what* is *that stink?*

He rubbed his nose as hard as he could, but nothing seemed to get rid of the smell.

Then he heard a sound—the feet of some large animal

behind him tromping across the cave floor.

He froze, pretending to be unconscious still. *Best not attract its attention.*

What sort of animal could be large enough to have carried him up from the beach to its lair?

What sort of animal smelled this bad?

Without meaning to, he shivered, remembering some of the tales his father had told. About giant cannibals, and boars big as houses. About monsters who ate the flesh off still-live men.

He slotted his eyes and saw a pair of hairy legs ending in cloven hooves. Not daring more, he had to be content with that one glimpse.

As the monster passed by, the stench went up Odysseus' nostrils like smoke up a chimney. It was all he could do not to choke.

Now the beast had moved entirely out of his line of vision. He could still hear it shuffling around, but until he could figure out what it was, he didn't want it to know he was awake.

Suddenly he noticed something strange. There was a thread of music, like a hummed tune, coming from one end of the cave.

Is there another prisoner in this cave as well? he wondered.

The shuffling feet came closer.

The smell got closer, too.

Odysseus squinted his eyes again, looking straight up

and into the round, snub-nosed face of a cheerful old grandfather leaning over him. The old man had a long, scraggly beard and thick, gray curls falling over his brow.

Relieved, Odysseus opened his eyes wide.

"Awake at laaaaast, eh?" the old man asked. His voice ended in a high bleat.

"Hsssst," Odysseus whispered. "The creature."

The old man looked puzzled, glanced around. "Whaaaaat creature?"

"Whoever carried me here . . ." Odysseus began. Then he sat up and stared at the old man.

At his bare arms and chest.

At his goat legs.

At the little horns poking through the gray curls.

"Time to eaaaat," bleated the goat-man.

Odysseus reached behind him for some kind of weapon—a loose rock, a club, a handful of sand—but there was nothing. So he did the only thing he could think of: he scrambled backward until he felt a cold stone wall behind him.

The creature shook its head. "Don't taaaaake on so, maaaanling," he chided. "Do mortals no longer remember old Silenus?"

"The satyr?" Odysseus had thought such creatures mere nursery tales.

"Aaaaat your service," Silenus said, then did a little capering dance on his goat legs, ending in a surprisingly graceful bow.

Odysseus was suddenly annoyed at being mocked by such a stinking, ugly creature. He stood, careful not to hit his head on the roof of the cave, and said, "I am Odysseus, prince of Ithaca."

The satyr's brow creased in thought. "Aaaaaa, yes—Ithacaaaa. Sour grapes. Ugly women."

"My mother—" Odysseus began.

"Aaaall men's mothers aaaare beautiful," Silenus said quickly. "Now eat? Or do you intend to follow drowning with staaaaarving? The gods cannot die. But a maaaan need not choose to die twice."

Odysseus suddenly realized he was not only terribly hungry but thirsty as well. "Water. I'd like water." He wrinkled his nose. "That is, if you have any."

"Here, maaaanling." The old goat-man held out a small wooden bowl filled with water.

Odysseus reached a bit tentatively for the bowl. Then he swallowed its contents down in a single gulp. "More."

Silenus got him another bowlful from a large pottery krater by the cave mouth. "Drink slowly, else you will bring it aaaaaall back up. Fresh waaaaater is in short supply on this island."

"I'd guessed that," Odysseus said, wrinkling his nose again. But in spite of the old satyr's advice, he drank the second bowl as quickly. And when he felt the water threatening to rise up, he calmed himself by closing his eyes and waiting for the spasm to pass.

"Now eat," Silenus said.

Odysseus watched warily, but when the old satyr passed him a large palm leaf heaped with nuts, berries, and boiled roots, Odysseus was suddenly so hungry, he quite forgot his host's smell. He devoured the humble meal as if it were a palace feast.

"Eat the leaf, aaaas well," Silenus said.

Maybe a goat can eat that, Odysseus thought, but all he said aloud was, "I thank you, kind sir, for the food and drink. I confess I was startled by your appearance."

"Staaaartled . . ." the satyr said, and smiled slyly.

"I wasn't afraid," Odysseus said, "if that's what you're thinking."

"Not aaaat all." Silenus nodded.

Before Odysseus could answer, something scuttered across the floor. The old satyr snatched up a club from somewhere behind him and brought it down with a loud *whack*. Smiling, he picked up the dead shrew by the tail. "Caaaare for seconds, young prince?"

Odysseus shook his head. Suddenly the nuts, berries, and water rushed up again, and he barely made it outside the cave in time.

Once his heaving stomach was emptied, Odysseus sat down in front of the cave mouth. It was quiet outside. Even the seabirds had grown silent.

The old satyr offered him a bowl of water, and this time Odysseus sipped it, making the single bowl last a long time.

Silenus dropped down beside him. Outside, the goat-man's stench was bearable.

Just.

"How caaaame you here?" Silenus asked. "I raaarely have visitors."

"Rarely?"

"Well, never before, aaaactually." He sighed, and his long beard fluttered.

Odysseus thought about telling the old satyr the truth about his escape from the pirates. But the truth was so unheroic. If he was to gain the satyr's coopera-tion, he'd have to impress it. He gave a moment's thought to what he would say and a deep crease grew between his eyebrows, but the creature didn't know the significance of that.

"I set out from Ithaca with five ships under my com-mand," Odysseus said, thinking five surely sounded better than one. And *my command* was grander than saying he'd been nursemaided by a merchant captain. "We sailed south to the land of the Egyptians, where we burned their cities and took their cattle, women, and gold."

Silenus leaned forward, his dark eyes bright with interest. "Is thaaaat where you injured your leg?"

"No, that was later," Odysseus said, really getting into the story now. "We were attacked by Poseidon's watch-dog, a great serpent of the sea. It swallowed my first ship, bit the second in half, and then started to pluck the men from my own ship one by one by one with its huge yellow teeth."

Silenus showed his own teeth, which were the color of sand.

"I seized my spear," Odysseus continued, "ramming it into the monster's neck, but not before one of the serpent's teeth gored me. Ignoring the pain, I ground the spear deep into the monster's flesh. It struggled frantically, and I was whipped off the deck and flung far across the sea, far out of sight of my comrades."

"Aaaaaaa," said Silenus.

Taking this for a sound of appreciation, Odysseus continued with grand gestures. "Seeing an island, I swam for it. And . . . here I am." He took a sip of the water. *Really,* he thought, *it* could *have happened that way.*

Silenus rubbed his beard. "Perhaaaaps," he baaed slowly, "customs have changed since I was maaaarooned here. Aren't you raaaaather young to be leading a waaaar baaaaand?"

"I am a prince," said Odysseus. "Do you doubt me?"

"You're right, maaaanling. What a poor host I aaaam to doubt aaaa prince's word. Or thaaat a prince's wound so recently gotten is aaaalready so well knit up."

Odysseus glanced down at the scar on his thigh, which was a dark line now, no longer the pulsing red of a new goring.

"Why should I question aaaaa story thaaat is the only real entertainment I've haaaad in my long exile?" The goat-man grinned.

Odysseus had the grace to look embarrassed. But only for a moment. "*Marooned*, you said. *Exiled*."

This time it was Silenus who seemed uncomfortable. "It was aaaa misunderstanding," he said. "Some nymphs. Too much wine. The usual thing. But I'm a saaaatyr. Whaaaat did they expect?" His voice rose in indignation. "How could I know this paaaarticular misunderstaaaanding haaaapened in Aaaaartemis' saaaaacred groves? No sense of humor, thaaaat one. None of the gods know how to laugh. Very full of themselves, they are. Aaaaartemis got her brother Aaaapollo to straaaand me here. A punishment. Long forgotten. On their paaaart. Not mine."

Odysseus finished drinking the water. "Haven't you even tried to escape?"

The satyr looked at him and shrugged. "Ever seen aaaa goat swim? I thought not. Still, perhaaaaps *you've* been sent by the gods to end my exile."

Setting the bowl down, Odysseus asked carefully, "What do you mean?"

"Follow me," said the satyr, standing.

Odysseus stood as well, but carefully. He didn't want to lose another stomachful of water.

Ambling in a rolling gait, the goat-man seemed entirely at ease. He led Odysseus along a small rocky ledge that jutted out over the sea. Odysseus had to pick his way with a great deal more care.

On the lee side of the path were stunted trees from which a single little wren was singing its own morning song.

"I caaaan work my passaaaage," Silenus was saying. "I'm aaaa good cook. Just drop me off aaaat the first convenient spot. Cytheraaaaa, perhaps, where delicious Aaaaphrodite first rose out of the sea. Or Naaaaxos." He smacked his lips. "Yes—it's faaaar too long since I saaampled the sweet Naaaaxos wine."

"What are you talking about?"

"Why—one of your ships is come to find you, O prince," Silenus said, beaming. "Look down there in the baaaay. You could tell them how I rescued you. You could taaaake me aaas aaaa paaaassenger."

Odysseus shielded his eyes from the sun that sparkled off the water. Where the satyr pointed, a ship lay on its side, pulled up onto the sand. A black-tarred ship. He recognized the fish markings on its side.

The pirates' ship.

CHAPTER TEN

THE PLAN

hey're collecting waaaater from the spring,"
said Silenus. "Been there since this morning.
But I was aaaafraid to show myself in caaaase—
like many maaaanlings—they're cruel."

"Crueler than the gods?" Odysseus asked.

"The gods do not eat goats," said Silenus.

Odysseus stared down at the busy scene below.

"You don't look very haaaappy," Silenus said. "I
thought you'd be haaaappy to see your shipmaaaates."

"That isn't my ship," Odysseus told him. "Those are
pirates."

"How caaaan you be sure?"

Odysseus sat back on his heels. "I've run into them
before."

"Before—or aaaafter—the fight with the sea serpent?"

Above them gulls flew in circles, screaming at one another.

Odysseus sighed. "There was no sea serpent."

Silenus nodded. "I knew thaaaat."

Odysseus said carefully, "Then know this: those pirates would cut my throat as well as yours."

"Aaaa," Silenus said. He flopped down onto a rock, with his elbows on his hairy knees. "I knew you weren't really aaaa prince. Moment I looked aaaat you, I knew. You're not taaaall enough. Not fine enough. Now Perseus—there was aaaa true prince. Aaand Hercules—the muscles on thaaaat boy. Aaand—"

"I *am* a prince," said Odysseus. "For what it's worth."

"Not worth much," the satyr said. "It's not princes we need now. We need aaaa hero."

"A hero!" Odysseus stood.

"Who is aaaa sailor," said Silenus, standing and sidling over to Odysseus, but thankfully downwind.

"I grew up around boats," said Odysseus. "I'm an islander, after all. I've sailed from one end of Achaea to the other."

Silenus looked suddenly sly. "If we found aaaa boat—even aaaa small boat—could you get us to the mainlaaaand?"

Odysseus rounded on the satyr. "You have a boat? Why didn't you tell me this before?"

"Well, it's a very *smaaaall* boat. Haaaardly worth

mentioning." Suddenly the sun hid behind a dark cloud, and the old satyr's face became full of shadows.

"How small?"

Silenus looked around, as if afraid of being overheard. "Some while back—months, years, I've lost count—this fishing boat waaaashed onto the beach. You'd be surprised—really you would—what I've found in the shaaaallows."

"Get on with it," growled Odysseus.

"It waaaas wrecked, of course. But I fixed it."

"So why haven't you sailed off?" Odysseus asked.

"Goats and waaaater. Baaaad mix. Baaaad. Baaaad. Baaaad."

Odysseus looked back over the ledge. There was an awning set up next to the pirate boat. He assumed the two girls lay under it. But he couldn't see Mentor anywhere.

"Where *is* your boat?" Odysseus asked suddenly.

"On the other side of the island," said Silenus. He joined Odysseus in looking over the ledge. "But we could taaaake *their* boat."

"You really don't know anything about ships, goatman," Odysseus said. "That's a full-size war galley. We couldn't even get it back into the water, let alone hoist the sail. We couldn't—"

Silenus sniffed loudly. "I smell something sweet."

"The wind must be blowing away from you then," Odysseus muttered, turned, and saw Mentor tied to a date tree.

He's alive! Odysseus bit his lip. *Thank you, Athena.*

"Wine and women, women and wine," sang Silenus, sniffing. "Nothing sweeter for paaaassing the time. . . ."

Odysseus grabbed the goat-man by the horns and pulled his head around to face him. "Listen, Silenus— I can sail your little boat. But first we have to rescue a friend of mine."

Silenus tore from Odysseus' grasp to look over the side again. "But there are two . . . twenty . . . thirty baaaad men there."

Odysseus yanked him back by the little goat tail. "Then we'll have to come up with a plan."

Making a plan was easy. Odysseus thought; it was a lot like telling a story.

Of course, in a story, heroes always win.

But acting on the plan was going to be a great deal more difficult. Large boulders, slippery rocks, and prickly bushes had their own way of adding to a tale. By the time Odysseus and Silenus were hidden among the rocks at the edge of the beach, Odysseus' arms and legs bore the scars of such a telling. His tunic was sopping wet with sweat, and the goat-man was—unbelievably—smellier than ever.

Still, they had gotten where they'd hoped to get: far enough away that the sailors couldn't hear them, close enough that they could watch what was going on.

It was clear the pirates were getting ready to leave.

The newly filled water jars were lined up by the side of the boat. Scattered about the beach were the remains of a cookfire.

Breakfast, Odysseus thought, and his stomach growled.

Mentor was no longer tied to the tree but now—bound hand and foot—he was propped against the ship's black hull.

A few yards away Helen and Penelope—also tied—sagged against each other. Helen had a gag over her mouth.

Odysseus wasn't surprised.

"Women," said Silenus by his side. "You didn't saaaay, but I knew. The nose aaaalways knows. Wine and women," he began singing in his bleating monotone. "Women and wine—"

Odysseus elbowed him. "Shut up. Go and do your part of the plan or you can forget about my helping you get off this island."

"I'll make my waaaay there and baaaack without them noticing," Silenus said. Then, casting one last lingering glance at the bound girls, he began to pick his way though the rocks with a speed and stealth Odysseus envied.

Just then the captain of the pirates stood, and in his stiff-legged mastiff way, walked over to the boat to check on things.

"Load the water first. Then the prisoners. Girls first.

Then push the ship off," he commanded loudly in his bark of a voice.

The pirates jumped to do his bidding. Odysseus was suddenly wondering if the satyr could possibly get to the other side of the beach in time, when a cry went up from one of the sailors.

"Look! Look!" A sailor with a curling beard was pointing.

The pirates all looked and, from his hiding place, Odysseus looked as well.

Silenus had indeed made good his boast. Hopping onto a large boulder, he started making obscene gestures in the sailors' direction. "Ugly sea dogs. Woof! Woof!" he cried. "Medusaaaa waaaas your mother. Ugly! Ugly! Like aaaa centaur's hind end!"

The pirates gaped at him.

Silenus did a little dance on the rock and stuck out his tongue. "Do the world aaaa favor," he called. "Behead yourselves. Baaaad men. Baaaaaaad." Bleating, he swung around bent over, and let loose a noxious blast of wind.

Boreas himself does not blow that hard, thought Odysseus with a grin.

The captain drew his sword. "After him, lads," he yelled. "But don't kill him. There may be some profit to be had from exhibiting that foul-tongued beast."

The pirates all swarmed off in pursuit.

Silenus had promised he knew every rock and crevice on the island and could easily shake off any pursuit.

Odysseus hoped this was true, for he needed plenty of time to free Mentor.

But at the edge of the beach, the pirate chief had a sudden change of heart.

"Thyetes," he called to one of the men, "go back and stay with those prisoners. Lest there be any more such beasties around."

Thyetes turned, his long, skinny legs carrying him back quickly to the boat, where he stood right beside Mentor. But instead of keeping an eye on the prisoners, he turned to watch his shipmates disappearing into the trees.

"Go on!" he cried after them, hoisting his spear. "Hit him once for me! No one says that about *my* mother!"

Odysseus hadn't counted on that. *What can I do?* he wondered. He looked around frantically. All that was near him was sand and stone and . . .

Stone.

He had a good throwing arm. Best among the boys at the palace in Ithaca. He could hit pretty much anything he aimed at. Bending down, he picked up two very large, smooth gray stones.

Odysseus took advantage of the pirate's turned back and heaved the first stone. It struck the pirate's shoulder, and he spun around, looking for the thrower.

Mentor saw Odysseus first, his eyes widening. Penelope saw him next. Helen was too busy muttering and straining against her bonds to notice anything but her own discomfort.

Just then the pirate spotted him and raised his mighty spear.

Twisting around, Mentor struck out with his bound-together legs and kicked the pirate in the knees.

"Ooof," Thyetes cried, beginning to fall.

Odysseus sprinted forward and brought the second stone down on the pirate's skull. The man dropped like a sack full of dates.

Plucking the pirate's dagger from his belt, Odysseus sliced through Mentor's bonds.

"I couldn't believe it when I saw you, galloping over the sand like . . . like . . ."

"Like a hero," Odysseus said, grinning.

"I meant like a ghost back unheralded from Hades."

"It takes more than a drowning to kill me," said Odysseus. "Can you stand?" He held out his hand and pulled Mentor up.

Mentor stood, though he was a bit wobbly from being tied up so long. "I can manage."

"We've got to get out of here."

"What about Helen? What about Penelope?" Mentor whispered, rubbing his chafed wrists.

"They're only women," Odysseus whispered back. "And they'll slow us down." The crease between his eyebrows suddenly appeared. "Once we're safely away and find our own ship, we can come back for them. Not now."

"But . . ." Mentor's face flushed. "We can't. . . . You don't mean . . ."

Odysseus seized his arm and pulled him away. "Think, Mentor, think," he said. "Helen is their big prize. They expect to make a handsome profit out of her. If we leave her, they'll probably sail on and deliver her to old King Theseus. And honestly—didn't you hear her before? She *wants* to go."

"Well, *I* don't want her to go," Mentor said. "Her *father* doesn't want her to go."

"She's a princess," Odysseus said, losing his patience and speaking loudly. "They marry old kings all the time."

"But . . ."

"If we take her now, the pirates will tear this island apart looking for her. *None* of us will get away then."

Penelope had heard the last part of their conversation. "He's right, you know," she told Mentor. "Go now. Rescue us later."

Mentor was about to argue with her, when he wrinkled his nose. "What's that awful smell?"

"Baaaad men aaaall gone," said Silenus, bounding over the sand toward them and waving his big wooden club. "I said I could do it."

"*What* is that?" asked Mentor.

"You mean *who* is that," Odysseus said. "Silenus, meet Mentor."

The two nodded at one another, each cautious in their greeting.

"He's got a small boat," Odysseus explained. "We'll lie low until the pirates leave and—"

"Women!" the satyr cried. Bounding past the two boys, he dropped his club, grabbed Helen, slung her over his shoulder, and loped back across the sand toward the shelter of the rocks.

CHAPTER ELEVEN

GOATS AND WATER

ou infernal creature!" Odysseus shouted, waving a fist at the fleeing satyr. "You've doomed us all!"

But Mentor wasted no time in cursing. Instead he was already racing across the sand in hot pursuit of Silenus.

Penelope held out her bound hands. "If you're going after Helen, you'd better take me as well. I'm the only one who knows how to cope with her."

Odysseus groaned but knew she was right. It was either take Penelope along now, or murder Helen later just to keep her quiet. He slashed through the ropes binding the girl's wrists.

"If we empty these water kraters, we can delay the

pirates' pursuit by boat," Penelope added. "They won't dare sail without stocking up again." She began kicking over the pottery jars until all but one spilled out their precious fluids onto the sand.

"Hurry," Odysseus said. "We have to catch Silenus before he and Mentor come to blows."

"Wait a minute," Penelope said, hefting the last heavy jar.

"Just kick it over and—"

"You really don't plan ahead very well, do you?" Penelope said.

"Of course I plan." Odysseus could feel heat rising to his cheeks. He was sure they were bright red. "How else do you think we managed to rescue you?"

"Rescue? Is *that* what you call it? Throw a rock and then run? And I bet that's as far ahead as you'd planned." She made a face. "Boys! Always thinking about heroics and never about what needs to happen day to day."

Odysseus began to sputter.

"If we're going to be in an open boat, my hero, we'll need fresh water ourselves." She staggered under the heavy krater, and at last Odysseus took it from her, settling it on one broad shoulder. Then he started toward the rocks.

When he looked back to see if Penelope was following, she was just stooping to pick up the dropped club, her long dark braids like thick ropes on either side of her face.

"Wait for me," she cried.

He slowed a bit, but his pride wouldn't let him wait.

They came upon the goat-man and Mentor about thirty feet beyond the rocks. The two were rolling about on the ground and cursing one another in steady streams of invective and bleating.

"Pillager!"

"Mortal!

"Goat from the hind end of Hades!"

"Boy whose paaaarts have not yet grown!"

Helen had been thrown to one side, where she lay with her skirts tumbled about her, the gag partially loose. Her disheveled curls perfectly framed her perfect face. She was crimson with outrage. And—Odysseus thought—very beautiful.

Penelope ran over to Helen and undid the bonds around her wrists. Then she ripped away the gag.

"My dress! My hair!" Helen screeched.

Penelope put her arms around her cousin for comfort. "There, there," she crooned.

Mentor now lay exhausted on the sand, but the satyr sat up and rubbed his head, between the little horns.

"You stupid creature," Odysseus said, setting down the krater of water. "You'll have brought the entire pirate crew down on our heads—and for what?"

The satyr drew himself up with a dignified air—or as dignified as a mussed-up, stinking, tangle-haired, bandy-legged goat-man could. "For the saaaake of a beautiful maiden," he said. "Surely we need a few comforts for the voyaaaage."

"*Comforts!*" screeched Helen. "I'll *comfort* you, you immortal dunghill. My brothers will pound you into paste. My father will skin you alive and use your hide for a rug."

Odysseus noticed that when Helen got going, she could turn a man to stone with her tongue. It certainly made the satyr wince.

"I thought she'd be graaaateful," said Silenus.

"Now you know why she wasn't part of my original plan."

But Mentor was now hovering over Helen, his hands waving in the air, as if he wanted to comfort her and didn't dare try. "Are you all right?" he asked. "Princess, are you all right?"

"Of course I'm not all right," Helen screeched. "Bad enough to be abducted by brigands. But then to be manhandled by a misshapen goat! Did you plan this as a joke? *Did* you?"

Behind her Penelope shrugged and put her hands into the air as if to say, *Even I can't solve this one.*

"Silenus has a boat," Odysseus said quickly, as much to silence the screeching girl as to inform her. "We're going to use it to get off the island and escape the pirates."

"A boat?" Helen looked over her shoulder at her

cousin, who smiled soothingly. "Why didn't you say so before?" She stood and smoothed down her skirt. "Take me there at once."

"Follow Silenus," Odysseus instructed the girls. "Mentor and I will bring up the rear." He handed the krater to Silenus, gave the knife to Mentor, and took the club from Penelope. "In case we're found," he said to Penelope. "That's how *boys* plan ahead."

Silenus hoisted the krater onto his shoulder and took off at a run. Hand in hand, Penelope and Helen went after him.

But Mentor turned, his lips tight together, a sure sign he was furious. "How could you let that brutish thing lay a hand on her?"

Odysseus sighed. "Whatever happened to 'thank you'?"

"He's a hairy, smelly *satyr*, Odysseus. Whatever were you thinking?"

"That hairy, smelly satyr took care of me when I could have died on the beach. That hairy, smelly satyr helped rescue you at great risk to himself. That hairy, smelly satyr has a boat." Odysseus' voice had gotten cold and old.

"What if he—"

Now Odysseus began to redden himself. "If you'd come when I told you instead of mooning over that vain little piece of Spartan honey cake, we'd be clear to the other side of the island by now."

"*Mooning!*" Mentor's face went gray. "I never—"

Odysseus put his hand over his heart and in a high whisper said, "Oh bea-u-te-ous maid, my heart flutters like the wings of a dove."

Mentor took a deep breath. "She can't help it if the gods have blessed her with surpassing beauty."

"I wish they'd blessed her with surpassing wisdom or a surpassing sword," Odysseus said.

Mentor pouted. "You don't know her like I do. She's been very nice since she found out that I'm a prince."

Odysseus said softly, "But you're *not* a prince, Mentor."

"Do we have to tell her?"

Odysseus didn't answer, but with a lift of his chin signaled Mentor to hurry on after the satyr and the girls.

"Hush," the satyr said suddenly. His sharp ears had picked up the sound of the pirates. Abruptly he changed direction, and the others followed him into a deep hollow, where they crouched shoulder to shoulder. Pulling a ragged bush down to cover them, Silenus put a finger to his lips.

Penelope was pressed up against the satyr as a kind of shield for her cousin. She made a valiant effort to hold her breath against his stink.

Helen whispered, "I'll never be clean again as long as I live."

"Shut up," Penelope said, managing to sound fierce and comforting at the same time. "Once we're back in

Sparta, you can bathe in asses' milk every day."

Just then they heard the pirates on the path, and they shrank even farther back into the hollow.

"How can anything that fat vanish into thin air?" asked one.

"It's more than I can fathom," said another.

"Come, let's return to the ship. That Spartan spitfire is still worth more than any goat-man," said a third.

The first one replied, "She'd better be. If the captain hadn't had her gagged, I wager he'd have had to throw her over the side or face a mutiny."

They laughed.

"Did you hear what she called Memnax . . . ?"

Their voices faded as they disappeared back around the bend of the path.

As soon as they were gone, Odysseus and the others climbed out of the hollow, pulling twigs and brambles from their clothes and hair. But Helen refused to move another step.

"I'm tired, dirty, and unhappy," she said. "I have been mauled, laughed at, and slandered."

Exasperated, Odysseus snapped, "Will you shut up and get going, princess? Once those pirates find that you and Penelope are gone too, they're going to be all over this island. Do you *want* us to be caught?"

Helen's eyes got narrow, and she glared back at him. "You rude, exasperating pig herder. I don't know how Prince Odysseus puts up with you, but my father will know how to deal with your insolence."

Odysseus was in no mood for games. "*I* am Prince Odysseus," he informed her. "And *he*"—he turned to glare at Mentor for a moment—"he is my companion, Mentor."

Unbelieving, Helen turned to Mentor who nodded and lowered his eyes in shame.

"Well . . ." she said, then she flounced off after the satyr.

Penelope just laughed and shook her head.

"You knew all along," Odysseus whispered.

"I guessed."

"And didn't tell her?"

Penelope shrugged. "Sometimes even a Spartan has to have some fun."

The satyr led them on tiny tracks that switched back again and again until at last they emerged into a small cove where a tiny two-man fishing skiff was sheltering under a stand of willow.

"There!" he said proudly. "The boat."

The hull of the skiff was crudely patched with wood and bark; the spindly pinewood mast looked scarcely strong enough to hold one of Helen's skirts, much less a linen sail.

"I'd sooner go to sea in that krater," Mentor said, pointing to the water jar.

"Where are the oars?" asked Helen.

"Is it supposed to haaaave oars?" The satyr's face collapsed in on itself with disappointment.

"How will we steer it?" Odysseus asked.

"I've paaaatched up the sail," said Silenus. "The wind can taaaake us where we will."

"Not unless you can tell the gods which way the winds should blow," Mentor said.

Penelope cocked her head to one side, considering. "Really, we don't have any choice."

"Of course we have a choice," Helen said firmly. "We can always go back to the pirates." She turned from them in a swirl of skirts. "They have a *proper* boat. And they don't smell like they just climbed out of a dung pile."

"Let her go if she wants," Odysseus said. "We haven't the time to argue with her."

Penelope turned on him. "For a hero you have an awful lot to learn about courage," she said. "I wouldn't abandon *you* to those cutthroats just to save my own life."

"My . . . own . . ." Odysseus sputtered and then, realizing he had no answer to what Penelope had just said, closed his mouth into a thin, firm slash. He walked over to the little boat and put his shoulder to the hull and began to push it toward the water.

"Wait!" Penelope cried. "The water jar!"

Silenus galloped to the boat and snugged the krater down next to the mast.

Mentor waded into the water and started pulling the boat from the water side.

Soon the little craft was afloat.

Odysseus called over his shoulder to Penelope. "You two girls, get onboard. Now."

Helen dug in her heels and shook her head, but Penelope took a firm grip on her arm.

"Just think how angry those cutthroats will be when they find we've escaped, Helen," she said.

Helen sighed, torn between pride and good sense.

"Come on," Penelope urged. "You know this boat is our best chance of seeing home again."

"Yes, that's what's so horrible," Helen said.

Penelope pushed Helen up into the boat and then she hauled herself in.

Mentor climbed in after, and Odysseus was next.

Leaning out over the stern, Odysseus held out a hand to the satyr, who was still standing on the rocky beach. "Come on, Silenus," he cried. "The tide is carrying us away."

The satyr put one hoof into the sea and paled as water surged up his leg. Gritting his teeth, he advanced one step, two, until his entire goat half was under the waves.

"Come on!" Odysseus shouted again.

Penelope took up the cry.

The satyr got as far as the boat and put his hands on the side. He tried to climb in, and the little skiff tilted alarmingly.

"He's going to drown us all!" Helen cried.

"Hush, cousin," Penelope said. "We're hardly three feet from shore."

At Helen's cry, Silenus had let go of the boat and fallen back into the water. He rose up out of the waves like some pitiable sea creature, wet strands of long gray hair hanging over his face.

"Silenus!" Odysseus cried out again. "Hurry!"

But the goat-man, coughing and spitting up brine, his body trembling in full panic, was already splashing back to the shingle. Once he reached the shore, Silenus turned a grim face to them.

"Don't be stupid, Silenus—the pirates will find you," Odysseus called to him.

"Don't worry, maaaanling," he bleated. "Goats and waaaater just don't mix."

The tide had now carried the boat too far out for the satyr to wade after them—even if he could have summoned up the nerve.

Odysseus lifted a hand in salute. "I will get a ship and come back for you," he shouted. "I swear it by the gods."

"Never swear by them, maaanling," came the return. "They taaaake themselves too seriously."

And then satyr and island were gone in one long swell of a wave.

CHAPTER TWELVE

SINGERS IN
THE MIST

he little boat shuddered with every new wave, but the patches held. The boys managed to raise the linen sail, which was as patched as the hull. A small wind teased into the sail, filled it, and—to their delight—the boat began to skim across the water.

"We're away!" Mentor shouted.

Screaming seabirds wheeled overhead, cheering them on.

Penelope grinned up at them, but Helen turned her head to one side and contemplated the endless sea.

It was some time later when Helen made her way to the little stern, where Odysseus and Mentor were taking turns trying to use the club as a makeshift steering oar.

"So," Helen purred to Odysseus, "*you* are the prince."

Odysseus nodded.

"And your father is king of Attica?"

"Ithaca. It's an island off the coast of—"

"I've never heard of it," Helen said dismissively. She pushed her curls back from her forehead. "Does he own a lot of ships?"

Odysseus paused to calculate. His father's fleet numbered about a dozen. "Quite a lot," he said.

"Well," Helen said, "my father is King Tyndareus of Sparta, and he has hundreds and hundreds of ships. Right now they're all scouring the seas for me."

"I wouldn't be so sure," Odysseus muttered.

Mentor cleared his throat. "Ummm, Helen, I come from one of Ithaca's noblest families. We have many slaves and many hectares of land, and my father fought at Thebes and—"

Helen sighed loudly, effectively silencing him. "How long have we been drifting, Prince Odysseus? It feels like forever."

Joining them, Penelope replied, "Only half a day. See—the sun is just past the—"

"I'm sure you're wrong," Helen said. "Otherwise I wouldn't be so hungry. And so thirsty." She reached for the water jar.

"You know we agreed on two swallows each a day, to conserve our supply," Penelope said, putting a hand over the top of the krater.

"Well, a drop then, just to moisten my face. Even the pirates allowed that. I'm turning into a dried olive."

"You look lovely to me," Mentor assured her.

Odysseus stifled a groan. He wasn't sure who he wanted to throw overboard first. Helen was insufferable, but Mentor was an embarrassment to Ithacan manhood. Only Penelope seemed to have any sense. Sense was what was needed on a voyage like this.

"Pig herder or prince," Penelope said suddenly, "what we *really* need is a good pilot. Do you have any idea where we are?"

Odysseus rubbed his chin and wished he were old enough to have started a beard already. He made a show of scrutinizing the horizon. There was no sign of land or a friendly sail, but at least the pirates had not caught up to them. Yet.

"From the sun's position, I believe we've been drifting southeast," he said with authority, though he hadn't any idea where they'd begun. A deep crease appeared between his eyes.

"Where will that take us?" Penelope asked. There was a look in her eye that told him she guessed how little he knew.

"Far away from anywhere we want to be," he told her honestly. He hadn't meant to say that. It just popped out.

"Great!" Helen said. She made her way to the front of the little boat.

Mentor followed.

The day dragged on and on. They were now so far from any land, there were no longer gulls calling above them.

Helen dozed, which at least meant that she was quiet. Mentor huddled near her, as if he could translate closeness into warmth. Penelope sat in the bow of the boat, keeping her own counsel. Odysseus was sure that she hated him. He wasn't sure he liked her very much, either. It's hard to like someone who has figured out your weaknesses.

There was little wind, and so the patchwork sail hung forlornly from the mast. The hot sun, the rocking waves, the silence in the sky soon had them all dozing fitfully.

Suddenly Odysseus jerked awake and gave a cry. Heading toward them was a wall of sea mist, looking like the gossamer skirts of a giant goddess. Something about the mist made him uncomfortable.

His cry wakened first Penelope, then Mentor.

Helen stirred slowly, her eyelids fluttering open. "What is it?"

"Just a sea mist," Penelope told her, as a thick fog enclosed the boat in its chilly, clammy embrace.

"These mist banks are never very large," Odysseus said. "We just have to wait them out." He sounded confident, but was not. He wished he could put a name to his unease.

Helen turned over and started to fall asleep again.

Just then a high-pitched keening came from inside the mist, a sound both joyous and despairing. One voice, then another, then another sang out. Soon the voices were all around them.

"Was that you singing, Helen?" Mentor asked. His eyes seemed strangely glazed. "Surely such a song could come only from lips such as yours."

Helen sat bolt upright. "Are you mad? My throat is parched. How could I possibly sing?"

"The singing, yes!" Odysseus cried. He had the same glazed look on his face. "It calls to me. Calls . . ." Getting up unsteadily, he started to put a leg over the side of the boat.

"No!" Penelope shouted. "Odysseus, what in Athena's name are you doing?" She seized him by the arm and yanked him so hard, he fell over onto his back.

"The song, the women, they're calling me," Odysseus said again in that same dreamy voice. He smiled up at the sky.

Letting out a sudden shriek, Helen made frantic shooing motion with her hands.

Penelope turned. "What is it?"

"There! There!" Helen screamed. "A woman's face. There. Now it's gone." She put a hand over her mouth, then took it away and screamed again. "Look! There's another."

This time Penelope saw it, too. A pale, sharp-featured human face, long black hair flying in the wind. A flash of a wing behind it, and it was gone.

"The song," Odysseus said again, starting to rise once more.

Penelope pushed him down again, then turned and grabbed Mentor's wrist, for now he was halfway over the stern. She threw him next to Odysseus. Neither boy put up much of a fight.

Helen grabbed Penelope's arm. "Are those things ghosts? Are we being haunted?"

"I think . . ." Penelope said, huffing a bit from the exertion. "I think they're sirens. Half woman, half bird. Honestly, Helen, don't you ever listen to the bards? The Argonauts battled sirens on their journey to get the Golden Fleece and—"

"I only listen to the love poems," Helen said, shrugging. "The rest is just boy stuff. Shields and spears and swords."

The keening was louder than ever, and wilder.

"Well, listen to *me* now. Sirens lure sailors to their death by singing. No man can resist them. Obviously neither can boys." She kept her foot on Odysseus' chest as he struggled once again to rise.

"Are you sure?" Helen asked. "Those sirens sound off-key to me. Father would never let them sing in *our* hall."

Penelope shook her head with exasperation. "Helen, it doesn't matter what they sound like to you or to me. To Odysseus and Mentor those songs are the most wonderful sound they've ever heard."

The boys both stood up together, and it took all of Penelope's strength to get them both shoved back down onto the bottom of the boat. All the while, the loud keening did not abate, and the boys struggled against her, though with little will.

"Helen, you've got to help me with these two, before they go and drown themselves," Penelope called over her shoulder.

"Why?" Helen asked. "Why should I care if they go overboard? They lied to me and spoke roughly and wouldn't let me have any water, and—"

"Because . . ." Penelope said, emphasizing each word, "we . . . don't . . . want . . . to . . . be . . . alone . . . in . . . the . . . middle . . . of . . . an . . . unknown . . . sea." She grimaced. "Neither of us is a sailor."

This argument finally moved Helen, and she sat down on Mentor's chest, crossing her arms and looking quite put out. "Well, if the Argonauts battled the sirens and won, how was it done?"

Penelope's brow furrowed as she tried to remember. With the constant keening around them, it was difficult to think.

She recalled the bard. He'd had one of those closed-in faces, his chin and cheeks freshly scraped free of any beard. When he told his stories to the accompaniment of the lyre, he had stared at the ceiling, and that made his throat apple bounce about. And . . .

Then she had it. "The great minstrel, Orpheus, was

aboard and he sang to the men. His song was stronger than the sirens' song."

Helen sniffed. "So we'll out-sing them then?"

"We can try," Penelope said. "Though I don't have much of a voice."

"My father," Helen mused, "claims I sing like a nightingale."

"Then sing, Helen!" cried Penelope as Odysseus once again began to struggle to his feet.

"Let me see," said Helen, "there's a spinning song my nurse taught me. Or the 'Wedding Hymn of Alcmene.' Or—"

"For the sake of the gods, cousin—this is not a performance. Just open your mouth!" Penelope cried.

Helen started to sing. Her voice was little more than adequate, and she could only remember bits of a dozen different songs. After a few lines of each, she gave up. "It's not easy singing out here with no one listening and throat raw and . . ."

Penelope had gotten behind Odysseus and kicked him in the back of the knees. As he sagged, she grabbed his tunic and pulled him over onto his back.

"I must go," he said muzzily. "They have prepared a lavish banquet." He sat up.

"Yes," Mentor added, in a soft voice. "Listen. There are sweet wines and soft beds. I must go, too." He pushed Helen off his chest.

"This is *not* going well," Penelope muttered, looking

around the little boat. Then she saw what she had to do. Loosing the rope, she yanked the sail down and wrapped it around them, first across Odysseus, then Mentor.

"Help me, Helen," Penelope said. "Wrap them till they can't move a muscle."

Helen got up and tried to tug at the linen folds, being careful of her nails. Finally, Penelope threw her on top of the boys.

"Just lie there. The combination of the sail and you might hold them for a while."

"But . . ." Helen began.

"And don't you dare whine, or I'll throw *you* overboard with them and sail off on my own." Penelope's voice was so tight, Helen feared she might actually do what she threatened.

The keening around the ship had gotten progressively louder, and now a woman's face once again appeared out of the mist. It was a predatory face, with a beaklike nose and sharp teeth. Behind that face beat strong wings, white as a gull's. The siren's voice pierced Penelope's ears like needles.

Picking up the club, she advanced on the singing creature and swung with all her might, smacking the bird-woman across the cheek. With a shriek of pain, the siren shot up and out of sight.

Another siren wheeled out of the mist, talons extended, and Penelope gave her a crack across the leg.

The siren winged off, squealing, and a third flew

down, took one look at Penelope waiting with the club, and spun away.

The mist around the boat disappeared all in a rush, and when it was gone, they were once again alone on the dark blue sea.

"What's going on?" Odysseus said, trying to disentangle himself from the sail and failing. "Are you idiots trying to suffocate us?"

Penelope pulled her cousin up and then bent to help the boys get free of the sail. "I was *trying* to save your life. Right now I can't remember why."

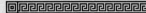

CHAPTER THIRTEEN

ADRIFT

ne day passed with Penelope carefully rationing the water.

Then a second.

The sun beat down on them, and they took turns resting in the little bits of shade offered by the krater.

By the third day, when they were all burned by the sun, hungry, cranky, sour-mouthed, and thirsty, Penelope said quietly, "There's no more water."

Her announcement was met with silence. No one was surprised, though Helen bit her lip to keep from crying out.

"Never mind, Helen," Penelope said. "Let's talk about Sparta. Listen—I'll sing you a song."

Mentor turned and stared out to sea, as if by looking

hard enough he might discover land.

Odysseus nodded, drifting into a half sleep, where he heard a faint echo of the sirens' song. When he woke, startled by Penelope's real song, he found himself angry. Angry at the boar, who had gored him and so sent him on this death's journey; angry at his grandfather, who'd hired an incompetent ship's captain; angry at the pirates for their brutal stupidity; angry at Silenus for salvaging such a fragile craft; angry at Mentor so entrapped by a girl's beauty that he was useless; angry at Helen, who'd surely sneaked more than her share of water. And mostly he was angry at Penelope for waking him.

Then he shook himself out of his anger.

In fact, Odysseus knew that Penelope was the one who'd saved them thus far with the krater of water and the club. It was Penelope who'd kept him—and Mentor—from diving overboard after the sirens. It galled him to admit it, but in her own womanish way, she was the *real* hero here.

And now she was standing and raising her arms.

"What are you doing?" Odysseus asked.

"The only thing left to us," Penelope said. "Praying to Zeus for rain." She looked up into the cloudless sky. "Father Zeus, lord of the storm, send us even the merest shower to lighten our sufferings. We will make sacrifices in your name when we're on land once again."

Not a cloud appeared in the sky.

"Silenus warned us not to rely on the gods," Odysseus

said. "Surely he knows them better than we do." *If anyone is to blame for this mess,* he thought, *it's the gods.*

Penelope looked over her shoulder at him. "I'm only asking for a little bit of water," she said. "A favor anyone would do for a thirsty stranger. If the gods refuse us, then the dishonor is theirs, not ours."

The hours dragged by and the girls slumped, shoulder to shoulder, at the front of the boat.

Odysseus couldn't sleep. He kept thinking about what Penelope had said. He'd never before considered that the gods might do something dishonorable. He just thought they were usually too removed from all human endeavor to actually care.

The very fact that it was a girl who'd given him something to consider made him uncomfortable. Girls, after all, became women. Women were meant to run the household, do the weaving, cook the food, raise the families. They weren't supposed to be onboard boats, fighting sirens, battling pirates—unless of course they were Amazons.

And neither Penelope nor her cousin Helen was an Amazon.

They were Spartans.

He turned to ask Mentor what he thought, but once again Mentor was staring at the sleeping Helen the way a drunkard stares into his wine cup.

"Hsst, Mentor!" Odysseus poked him in the small of the back.

Mentor turned his sunburned face toward Odysseus and forced a smile. "Hsst, yourself. Have you a plan at last?"

"No plan yet. But there's something I want to ask you. It's about girls. And women."

"Isn't Helen wonderful?" Mentor had that dreamy look again.

Disgusted, Odysseus forgot everything he'd just been thinking and blurted out, "I think she's a sorceress."

"How can you say that?"

"Because she's made a slave of you without the use of chains or bonds."

Mentor sighed. "No spells are necessary, Odysseus. It's her beauty that so affects me."

Odysseus drew himself up. "Oh, she's comely all right. If she were a slave girl on sale at the market, I *might* consider purchasing her. But you've let her unman you completely."

Mentor turned to face Odysseus directly. "Odysseus, we're inches from dying. Is it wrong for me to want her to find me worthy of her love before we cross over to the Underworld?"

"You're supposed to worry about being worthy in the eyes of the gods, in the eyes of your fellow men—not a mere woman. What matters is your courage. Your honor." He struck himself on the chest.

"What honor is there in drifting in a boat, Odysseus?"

Actually, Odysseus had been wondering that same thing himself. "At least . . ." he began, "at least I can die on this boat without complaining, facing death with courage. Otherwise, what will I say when I face the judges of the Underworld? If we haven't been worthy, how can we hope to enter the paradise of the Elysian fields? We'll be forced to wander the gloomy caverns of Tartarus forever."

Mentor said nothing.

"Square your shoulders, Mentor. Head high. No more mooning over Helen. Let's be true comrades laughing in the face of death." He leaned toward his friend, hoping he had succeeded in bringing him to his senses. "Mentor?"

Mentor's answer was a deep, rhythmic snore.

The next day they were all so exhausted from sun and hunger and thirst, they hardly spoke. Helen even stopped complaining.

One by one they dropped off into a semisleep. Odysseus was the last. But he woke suddenly, startled by the sensation of water trickling over his toes, then came completely awake.

The crude patches Silenus had used to repair the little boat were peeling apart, and seawater was seeping through the cracks.

"Get up!" Odysseus shouted. "Up! Up! Up!"

The others lifted heavy eyelids and roused at the sight of the seawater, which already covered the bottom of the boat.

"The jar!" Penelope shouted, and Odysseus began bailing with the krater, but the water came in as fast as he threw it out.

"This is the end of us!" Helen wailed. "One of you must have offended the gods."

"If the gods so love *you*, why haven't your father's ships found us yet?" Odysseus countered.

For a moment Helen seemed poised to answer. Then she buried her face in her hands and sobbed.

Penelope glared at him, and Odysseus flushed, as ashamed as if he'd struck down an unarmed enemy from behind.

"Perhaps . . ." croaked Mentor. "Perhaps one of them *has* found us." He pointed. "Look!"

There was a tiny outline of a ship far off in the hazy distance.

"But the wind is taking us away," Helen pointed out.

Swiftly, Odysseus untied the sail and pulled it down, wadding it into a bundle, which he threw over into a corner of the boat.

"Are they getting closer?" Helen asked.

"They don't seem to be moving at all," Penelope said.

"Then we're just going to have to swim for it," Odysseus told them. "Before they get under way again."

"I can't," Helen said bluntly.

Odysseus rolled his eyes. "Swimming isn't going to mess up your dress or hair any more than they are already."

Helen turned her back on him, but Penelope put a hand on his arm. "Helen was never taught to swim," she said. "It wasn't considered ladylike."

"And you?" Odysseus asked.

She smiled wryly. "No one's ever accused me of acting like a lady. But I can't leave Helen here."

"All right, then, *I'll* swim," said Odysseus. "And if the ship's crew looks friendly, I'll have them pick you up."

Before he could go over the side, Penelope said, "Don't be silly. You're in no better shape than the rest of us. We haven't come this far to see you drown because of some stupid heroics. We need to do something more practical."

"Like pray to the gods?" Odysseus asked sarcastically.

"No. First spread the sail over the floor of the boat. That might just keep water from coming in. Then we can use the mast as an oar."

With Mentor's help, Odysseus wrenched the mast out of its socket. Meanwhile the girls stuffed the sail against the loosened patches.

Then the boys sat side by side on a bench, holding the mast. As it wasn't much longer than Autolycus' hunting spear—though a great deal thicker—they were able to draw it through the water, first on one side of the boat, then the other.

Gradually the little boat began to move.

"At this rate, that ship will be gone before we get there," said Odysseus, not stopping to wipe sweat from his eyes.

"I don't think so," Penelope said. "There doesn't seem

to be any sail hoisted. And there's no sign of movement."

She picked up the jar and began bailing while the boys propelled them slowly but surely toward the other ship.

An hour went by. Then another. But they grew closer and closer until the ship loomed before them, only a few yards away.

First Mentor, then Odysseus lifted their blistered hands from the makeshift oar. Their backs ached, too.

Now that they were close, they could see that there was no visible mast, and the boat's oars trailed lifelessly in the water.

"Halloooo," Odysseus shouted up.

No one answered his hail.

"Halloooo," they all cried together.

Still there was no answer.

"Why hasn't anyone seen us yet?" Mentor asked.

"Halloooo," Helen called by herself. "Anyone up there? Help!"

The sides of the hull were so high, it was impossible to catch sight of the crew.

"Perhaps," Penelope said slowly, "it's a plague ship."

"Then it'd mean possible death to board her," said Mentor.

"It means *certain* death if we stay here," Odysseus said, pointing to the puddle of water spreading around his ankles.

CHAPTER FOURTEEN

THE MYSTERY SHIP

T he water was now leaking into the little boat faster than they could bail it out.

"What can we do?" Helen wailed, hoisting her skirt above her knees in a vain attempt to keep it dry.

Odysseus examined the oars of the mystery ship. Each stuck out at exactly the same angle from holes halfway up the side of the ship, the oar heads dimly visible under the water. Taking hold of one, he found that it was as firm as if it had been set in a rock.

"I think . . ." he said, "I think it's climbable. At least— I hope it is." He drew in a deep breath. "I'll go first. And if it's safe . . ."

He didn't wait to hear any arguments, for even a small hesitation on his part was going to puncture his resolve. He immediately clambered onto an oar. When it didn't collapse under his weight, he crawled gingerly up its entire length. Once at the hole where the rest of the oar disappeared into the dark bowels of the ship, he stood up carefully and stretched till his fingers curled over the upper edge of the ship's hull. With a heave and a grunt, he hauled himself up and rolled onto the deck. Then he kissed the flooring and sat up.

He was glad none of his friends could see his face, where fear was now dissolving into relief. But just as suddenly fear returned. What if the *crew* had seen him?

Yanking the pirate's dagger from his belt, he darted quick glances around the ship.

No crewmen.

No monsters.

No ghosts.

In fact there was no sign of life at all.

Carefully keeping a watch around him, Odysseus explored the entire deck. Not only was there no mast, there wasn't even a sign of a socket where a mast might be fixed.

By the stern, under a tan-and-white striped linen canopy, he found three kraters of water, four jars of preserved fruit, and a basket of dry bread. There was also a length of coiled rope.

Odysseus picked up one of the water jugs and drank greedily. Then he picked up the rope and went back to the side of the ship where his companions waited in the sinking boat.

Waving, he called down to them, "There's no one here at all. But there's water and food and—"

"Get us up there!" Helen cried.

For once the others agreed with her.

Mentor was the last to climb over the side, and when he looked back, Silenus' little waterlogged boat was finally swamped by a succession of white-capped waves.

"Just in time," he said as he untied the rope from his waist.

The girls were already drinking water and laughing as if drunk on wine. When Odysseus and Mentor joined them, Penelope handed them each a loaf of dry bread. They ate the loaves without a complaint, washing them down with great gulps of water.

Then they flopped down under the canopy and feasted on the preserved fruits as if they were at a grand banquet.

"What else is there?" Mentor asked. "I could eat a centaur and still be hungry. Do you suppose there's any meat? Or olives? Or—"

"No more for me," Penelope said. "My stomach must have shrunk to the *size* of an olive. It has had enough."

Helen burped prettily, putting her hand over her mouth.

"Look around," Odysseus said, leaning back against a large pillow and waving his hand at Mentor. "Whatever you find, it's yours! I'm as full as Penelope."

Mentor made a mock bow. "Thank you, great lord." He began to root around behind the jars of water and fruit. "More bread," he said, "drier than the last." He pushed aside another jar. Behind it was a white cloth packet lying against the planking. "What's this?"

Odysseus sat up, and Penelope did, too. Only Helen, eyes closed, seemed more interested in sleep than mysteries.

"Give it to me," Odysseus said.

"You told me that whatever I found was mine," Mentor said.

"I meant food."

"Did not."

"Did, too."

Penelope snatched the packet from them. Carefully she unwrapped the cloth. Inside was a large golden key with a pointed piece at the end. She bit it. "Gold clear through."

"Why would anyone make a key out of gold?" Odysseus mused.

"Gold? Key?" Helen sat up, suddenly interested.

Odysseus took the key and held it up to the light. "What do you think these mean?" He pointed to some strange markings on the side.

Penelope snatched the key back and studied it closely. "It's called script. A kind of writing. Don't you know how to read?"

"What does one need writing for?" asked Mentor. "We've signs to keep track of our stock of grain, to assign weapons to our warriors, to record tribute. What else does a kingdom need?"

Odysseus nodded.

"Well, script is more useful than that," Penelope told them. "These markings don't represent *things*, like your picture signs do. Each of these"—she pointed to the markings on the key—"is a sound. When you join the sounds together, they make words. You can send greetings, tell stories—"

"Bards tell stories," said Mentor. "No need to write them down."

"Words?" Odysseus squinted his eyes and stared carefully at the key. "What words?"

"Well, in this case, a name," said Penelope.

"What name?" Helen asked.

Penelope ran her finger across the strange script. "Dae-da-lus. Daedalus."

"Never heard of him," Odysseus said.

"Of course you have," Mentor said. "He was a great craftsman and toy maker. Served King Minos of Crete for many years. Built the Labyrinth, the maze where the monstrous Minotaur, half bull and half man, was imprisoned. Don't you remember, Odysseus? The bard at your father's house sang about him the evening before we sailed off to your grandfather's."

"Oh—the monster. I remember *that* part. I wasn't much interested in the craftsman, though. Or the toy maker."

Helen shuddered deliciously. "A monster?"

"Oh yes, a horrible monster," Mentor said, turning to her. As she trembled again, he expanded on the story, clearly trying to impress her. "The people of Athens were forced to send a tribute of youths and maidens to King Minos, and he shoved them into the maze where they were devoured by the Minotaur."

Helen put her hands over her ears. "Don't tell me any more."

Mentor pulled her hands away. "Sweet Helen, the Minotaur was killed long ago. No need to worry about it now."

Odysseus rolled his eyes. "Enough! What do we need old tales for when we are right in the middle of an adventure of our own?"

"*Adventure?* Is that what you call this?" Helen said.

Penelope agreed. "We almost died out there in the satyr's boat."

Odysseus laughed and took the golden key back from Penelope, tying it onto the thong that held his bronze spearhead. He tucked them both inside his tunic for safekeeping. "Any danger averted is an adventure. *If* you live to tell the story."

"We're not on dry land yet," Penelope reminded them all.

After an hour's rest, they fell to eating again, but Odysseus was restless. He drummed his fingers on the deck.

"What is it?" Mentor asked.

"This ship. It puzzles me. I don't like what I can't understand," Odysseus said. "There's no mast. No sail. We can't get at the oars. If there ever was a crew, how were they supposed to row anywhere?"

"Good questions," mused Mentor.

"I'm just grateful we aren't at the bottom of the sea," Helen said.

Penelope shook her head. "No, Helen, Odysseus is right to wonder. If we just sit here, becalmed, until the supplies run out, we're hardly any better off than we were before."

"Except that the boat isn't sinking," Mentor pointed out.

"So we die of starvation instead of drowning. Neither death gets us to the Elysian fields," Odysseus said.

"Is that all that men worry about?" Helen asked sharply.

"Look, that golden key must have been left for a purpose," Penelope said. "Let's see if we can find a keyhole."

"A keyhole!" They all stood.

"I'll take the front of the boat," said Penelope.

"The bow," Odysseus said.

"You can take the back," she added, ignoring him.

"The stern," Odysseus said.

"And Helen the right side—"

"Starboard."

"And Mentor—"

"Port side. Left."

Penelope made a face at him, but it was clear she was also storing away the words for later.

They each went to their appointed places. Penelope and Mentor searched with painstaking slowness, inch by careful inch. Helen lingered by the side of the ship, often staring out at the vast blue-green sea, with its white-capped waves.

Meanwhile Odysseus began his search at the extreme end of the stern.

Think, he cautioned himself.

He noted that there was no great oar for steering the ship.

Very strange, he said. *So how does the boat stay on its course?*

He found a wooden shaft reinforced with bands of metal sticking out of a dark slit in the deck.

Even stranger.

He touched the shaft tentatively. It was solid. He tried to pull it up, but it remained as firmly rooted as an oak. When he leaned against it, to his surprise it moved stiffly from one end of the slit to the other.

Strangest of all!

The shaft locked into place with a loud *click*. After that, no amount of pushing or pulling on his part could shift it again.

He grunted in disgust and had just turned his back on the useless thing when a great tremor ran through the ship.

Helen screamed.

"What's happening?" cried Mentor.

"What did you do, Odysseus?" Penelope called.

"Nothing," he said, a small line beginning between his eyes. "Except . . ." He was just thinking that he'd better tell them about the lack of steering oar and the strange shaft and the stiff movement, when his voice was suddenly drowned by a noise that shook the deck beneath their feet.

Helen and Penelope clapped their hands to their ears. Mentor tried to shout over the noise.

But Odysseus stood still, head to one side, puzzling out the sound. He'd heard a noise like that once before, when his father had ordered an inventory of his armory. Spears, swords, shields, breastplates had been stacked into heaps. The clang of metal on metal had resounded throughout the palace for three days.

It's almost as if we're standing on top of the god Hephaestus' workshop, Odysseus thought.

As suddenly as it had begun, the clanging and crashing ceased. There was a moment of stillness so intense, the four of them didn't dare to breathe.

And then, without warning, the ship lurched into motion as the great oars began to cleave the water with powerful strokes.

The four scrambled to the right side of the ship.

"Starboard," Penelope whispered, looking down as the oars moved in perfect unison.

Slowly the vessel turned, swinging about in a great half circle. Then it set off across the endless expanse of sea.

"What could have started the ship?" Helen asked, still staring at the perfect precision of the oars.

Odysseus sighed so loudly, they all turned to him. "I pulled a rod in the back of the boat."

"The stern," Penelope said.

He ignored her. "It went from one side to the other and then something gave a loud click. That's when the ship began to move. Perhaps the rod was some sort of signal."

"A signal to whom?" Mentor asked uneasily.

"About what?" asked Penelope.

"And why?" Helen's voice was unusually quiet.

They could feel the gentle vibrations beneath their feet. At the same time there was a regular, metallic beat below the deck, like a smith hammering a blade into shape.

"Someone has to be down there working the oars," said Mentor.

"Or some *thing*," Helen said. She shivered.

"Slaves?" asked Penelope.

Odysseus shrugged. "Why aren't there any voices? How are they fed? Who brings them water? Who guards them?" Odysseus ran out of questions.

"Maybe it's not slaves," said Helen. "Maybe it's monsters." She shivered. "Or ghosts."

"*Whatever* it is—we need to find out," Odysseus said.

"Why?" Helen asked again.

"Because we need to know who's rowing. And where we're going," Penelope told her.

"We searched the ship," Mentor pointed out. "The only thing we found was the signal rod."

"We searched the *sides* of the ship," Penelope pointed out. "We didn't search the floor."

"Deck," said Odysseus, but he nodded. Without waiting for the others, he dropped to his hands and knees and began crawling along the deck, checking out every crack and line in the boards.

Penelope joined him and, a bit more reluctantly, so did Mentor. Helen turned away from them to stare again out to sea.

It took a long time for them to crawl the entire deck, but at last Mentor cried out, "Here!"

He straddled a barely visible square near the ship's bow.

The others ran over to see what he had found.

"Is it a hatch?" Mentor asked.

"What's a hatch?" asked Penelope.

"A door into the ship's hold," Odysseus said.

"What's a hold?" she asked.

"There's no handle," Helen pointed out. "How can you open it without a handle?"

Odysseus drew his dagger and knelt down. "With this." He forced the point into the right side of the thin crack.

"Don't!" Helen cried, putting her hands on his shoulders. "You don't know what's down there. You might be freeing the souls of dead sailors. You might set a monster loose. You might—"

"Isn't it better to know than to sit here and tremble?" asked Odysseus, shrugging off her hands.

"Trembling is better than dying," Helen whispered, clasping her hands to her breast.

Odysseus didn't answer her. Instead he began to prize up the hatch, just enough so that Mentor could catch the edge. Then together the boys hauled the heavy door open, grunting as they worked.

The metallic noise grew louder, and an oily smell wafted up from below.

Odysseus stuck his head down through the opening.

"Is it a hold?" Penelope called. When he didn't answer, she added, "What do you see?"

There were small points of illumination coming from the oar holes. That light was enough to see that the hold was full of wheels.

Metal wheels with notches.

Notches fitting into other notches.

Long bronze rods moving between the wheels.

Odysseus sat up. "It's as though the metal itself is alive."

"Or some invisible monster is at work," cried Helen.

"Or spirits of the air moving the wheels," Mentor added.

Penelope folded her arms and bit her upper lip. "Perhaps it's some intricate toy built by Daedalus himself." She looked cautious. "We'd better not tinker with it."

Reluctantly Odysseus agreed. "Whatever it is—monster-run or spirit-driven or master toy, if we go down there and stop it, we might not get it started again. And then we could be becalmed here forever." With Mentor's help, he set the hatch cover back down.

"So now what?" Mentor asked.

"We eat," said Odysseus.

"We drink," said Helen.

"We wait," Penelope added. "But not, I hope, too long."

CHAPTER FIFTEEN

THE LONG ISLAND

All that day the boat continued moving, and the four took turns watching the water, hoping for ships, for gulls, for land, for anything to break the monotony of sea and sky.

Odysseus took the longest watches. The food and water had filled him with energy, and there was nowhere else to expend it. Awake, he gave a lot of thought to the mystery ship. Wherever it was taking them, he'd no doubt the destination would be just as strange and intriguing as the vessel itself.

Leaning against the prow, scanning the sea, Odysseus was riveted on the horizon when Penelope came to stand beside him.

"My turn," she said, touching him lightly on the arm.

"I'd rather watch here than look after your cousin."

She smiled wryly. "Mentor is doing that ably. He's telling her all about Ithaca, and she's just bored enough to listen."

Odysseus gave a short bark of a laugh. "How do you put up with her? I'd have thrown her over the side of the ship by now if you weren't here."

"And how brave would that make you then?"

Odysseus sighed. "I'm not trying to start an argument."

"Neither am I," Penelope said. Her face softened. "But I'm trying to make a point. *You* were raised a warrior. Adventure has been bred into you. Helen was raised to be beautiful and pampered and spoiled. It's not her fault that she can't face danger with a hero's heart."

"But you," Odysseus said carefully, rubbing a hand through his thick red hair, "you're not like that. And as a princess of Sparta yourself, surely you were raised the same way."

"My looks never invited such a spoiling."

"You're handsome enough," Odysseus said. Then he looked away, embarrassed about delivering a compliment.

"Thank you," she whispered to his back, not caring if he heard. "But no one is in Helen's class."

Odysseus turned to face her again. "So who pampered and spoiled her then?"

"Everyone," said Penelope. "Her father most of all. If

she's desired by every king and noble in Achaea, she becomes worth more to him than gold or jewels. He can use her beauty and desirability to make any king his ally."

Odysseus turned back to gaze at the endless length of the dark sea. Suddenly he leaned forward, squinting his eyes. "Look!" he cried.

Penelope turned around and stared. "What am I supposed to see?"

"Land!" Odysseus shouted. Then to be sure that Mentor and Helen had heard as well, he cried out again. "There's land ahead!"

They raced over to see.

"What land is it?" Mentor asked.

"Egypt?" hazarded Penelope.

"Too mountainous for Egypt," Mentor said.

"We've been sailing west, not south," said Odysseus. "My guess is it's the Long Island." There was an eager gleam in his eye.

"I hope not," Mentor said. He stared straight ahead.

"Why do you say that?" Helen asked. Now she, too, leaned over the ship's side and stared ahead.

"Well, because . . . because it's a long way from home."

"But at least it's land," Helen said. Then she turned and went back to the shelter of the canopy, where she began running her fingers through her hair like a comb.

As soon as Helen was too far away to hear, Penelope rounded on the boys. "What is *really* wrong with this Long Island?"

"The Long Island is what we Ithacans call Crete," Odysseus said.

"King Minos' island? Where the monster was in the maze?" Penelope nodded. "That makes a kind of sense. Daedalus made a ship that takes us straight to Crete, where once upon a long time ago he made a maze to hold a monster. But . . ." She thought a minute. "You said the monster in the maze is dead."

The boys looked quickly at each other.

"It *is* dead—isn't it?" Penelope asked.

"Very dead," said Mentor. "But . . ."

"But what?" Penelope asked, hands on her hips.

"Sailors' tales," Odysseus said. "That's all. Men who are too long at sea like to make up stories."

Penelope was not to be fobbed off with that answer. She'd already noticed that when Odysseus told a lie, a vertical line grew between his eyes. The line was there now. "*What* stories?"

"Other . . . kinds of monsters," Mentor said at last. "But none that are to be believed."

She was unable to tell whether they were speaking the truth or cushioning her from fear, so she looked instead at the land that was coming nearer with every stroke of the oars.

It was clearly a very, very long island, and as the ship drew closer, a great cliff face reared before them. The four now stood shoulder to shoulder, watching.

"The oars don't seem to be slowing down," Mentor noted with a worried expression.

"We'll all be dashed to pieces on the rocks," Helen cried.

"I don't understand," Penelope said thoughtfully. "Is the ship trying to destroy itself?"

"Us," Helen screamed. "It's trying to destroy *us*!"

Grabbing her cousin's shoulders, Penelope said very clearly, "Listen, Helen—if the ship had wanted to kill us, it need never have picked us up in the first place."

Helen's beautiful blue eyes widened. "But it didn't pick us up. We found it!" The eyes began to pool.

Penelope's face scrunched up, and she stared down at her feet.

"Maybe we should jump off and swim to shore," Mentor said.

Odysseus had been silent through this frantic conversation, trying to gauge wind and water, trying to make sense of the oars' tireless drive through the sea. At last he turned to the others.

"There's one thing we *can* do," he said. He went back to the canopy and returned with the satyr's club. "Help me open the hatch again, Mentor. I'll go down there and smash the ship's innards. That should kill it."

"No!" Penelope cried, grabbing his arm. "Who knows what could happen to you down there."

"Nothing worse than what will happen to all of us up here if the ship rams those cliffs," he said.

Shrugging off her grip, Odysseus once again pried

open the hatch with his knife. Mentor helped him lift the door, which seemed even heavier this time. They gazed down into the ship's fearsome belly, where rods and wheels pounded and creaked relentlessly.

Then they both sat back on their heels.

Odysseus spoke first. "If this doesn't work, make sure you all jump *before* the ship hits the cliffs. Grab some wreckage to keep you afloat till you find a safe stretch of shore."

Mentor glanced quickly at Helen, who was staring mutely at the fast-approaching rock face. "Let *me* go down into the hold," he said. "You're a prince. She's not interested in me."

Odysseus smiled. "I'd rather die down there than have to swim your princess to shore. She's all yours."

He took hold of the edge of the hatch and was just preparing to lower himself down when Penelope cried out. "Wait! There's a gap in the rock!"

Odysseus leaped up, and he and Mentor ran to where Penelope stood, pointing. Helen came, too.

"There! There!"

A dark sliver, a narrow canyon, was barely visible in the gray rock wall.

Mentor squinted and shook his head. "It's too narrow. The ship will never make it through."

"The ship seems to think it can," Penelope said.

Instinctively, they all retreated to the stern, linking arms.

Just then there was a loud clanking, and the oars suddenly tipped upward till they were pointing toward the sky. Catapulted by a large wave, the ship sped forward through the gap, and into a darkness blacker than any night.

Helen screamed.

And then the others—even Odysseus—screamed with her.

CHAPTER SIXTEEN

THE BRONZE GUARDIAN

"**I** knew this was a death ship," Helen moaned. "Knew it the minute I saw it. Surely we've found the Underworld, and this is the River Styx." In the pitch black her voice seemed much too loud.

Odysseus wanted to dismiss her fear, but any words of comfort stuck in his throat.

"Perhaps it was Hades himself who made the ship. To steal me away as he stole Persephone," Helen continued. Her voice was strangely calm, as if such a fate were almost appealing.

"Not *everything* that happens in the world hinges on you, Helen," Penelope said with sudden anger.

Just then the ship made a deep turn, and they emerged

back out into the light. They could see they'd just traveled through a narrow cave that opened into a small bay. Ahead the shoreline was studded with jagged rocks rearing up like monstrous fangs. Thrusting from the midst of the fangs, like a giant tongue, was a stone jetty.

"Not the Underworld then," Penelope said dryly.

"Not yet," Odysseus said.

The ship showed no sign of slowing down, and they were heading so fast toward the rocks that none of them doubted that the ship would be dashed to pieces. Wordlessly, they each grabbed on to the ship's sides, ready for the fatal impact.

At the last possible moment, the oars snapped down, back-paddling, the flat of the blades set firmly against the wave. A huge spume cast up on either side, filling the ship with spray. In an instant, the momentum of the ship was stopped so suddenly that the four passengers were thrown forward.

Penelope's head cracked painfully on the deck, and Helen became so tangled in her skirts, she looked bound. Odysseus did a rolling flip. Mentor was flung into the air, landing on the boards like a fresh-caught fish.

For a long moment none of them moved.

Then Helen moaned.

Raising his head, Odysseus was the first to realize that the ship had stopped. He pulled himself up and looked over the side. They were only a few yards from the rock pier.

Glancing up at the sky, he said aloud, "I hope you gods are enjoying the joke." He gave Penelope a hand, then Helen. At last he started over to Mentor.

"I'm all right," Mentor said, though a large bruise was already purpling the side of his knee. He stood without help.

"Can you walk?" Odysseus asked.

"If I have to, I can even run," Mentor answered.

"I suggest running, then," Penelope said. "Before the boat changes its mind and carries us back out to sea."

Odysseus went first, dropping over the side into thigh-high water. He held his arms out, and Mentor helped first Penelope, then Helen down, and Odysseus caught them.

At last Mentor jumped too, a grimace on his face when he landed on his bruised leg.

They waded to the stone pier and looked back at the ship, still riding high in the water.

"I wish . . ." Odysseus began. For a moment he was silent.

"*What* do you wish?" Penelope asked.

"I wish . . ." He couldn't say it aloud for fear that Penelope would laugh, but what he wished for was more time on the ship, to learn its controls. Such a ship might carry him tirelessly to the ends of the earth. Instead, he turned to Penelope and said, "I wish we could get somewhere dry and warm."

"Yes, Prince Odysseus! Yes!" Helen cried. "What

about that tunnel over there?" She waved dramatically at a sea cave to their left.

"There's water in that," Mentor pointed out. "Hardly dry and probably not warm either."

Penelope stared at Odysseus oddly, head cocked to one side, as if able to read the *real* wish on his face. Then she turned away, stared up at the cliff, and suddenly shouted, "Look! Up there."

A door of polished bronze with great incised pictures across the lintel was set right into the cliff face.

Odysseus wasted no time in wonder. He scrambled up a narrow pebble path toward the doorway, the others following right behind.

Closer up, the door was even stranger. The picture over the lintel showed a monster—half bull and half man—standing over a dozen dead children.

"The Minotaur," Mentor said.

Odysseus controlled a shudder. Some of the children in the picture looked to be his age.

"There's no keyhole," Penelope said.

Odysseus placed his shoulder against the door and pushed with all his might, but the door didn't budge. Mentor came over to help, but still the door didn't move.

"I don't think this door's meant to be broken through," Mentor said. "At least not by us."

"Maybe we should go back to the ship," Helen suggested. "We have food there and water and—"

"Wait!" Penelope had found a small hole in the rock

next to the door and poked her little finger in. "Do you think the key goes here?"

Odysseus pulled the key and spearhead from his tunic. He touched the script on the key with his fingers. "Dae-da-lus," he whispered, as if reading it. Then he inserted the long nose of the key into the hole.

It fit exactly.

"Turn it!" Helen shouted, clapping her hands. "Turn it!"

Odysseus turned the key. Something shifted noisily inside the rock, like the sound in the hold when the oars first began working.

"Daedalus," he said aloud. "Old toy maker. What kind of toy is this?"

The door sprang inward, and Mentor, who was still leaning against it, fell backward into the rock.

Odysseus picked him up and, going first, walked into the shadowy passageway. Twenty steps along, where the light from the doorway did not penetrate, he came to a stop.

The others caught up.

"What is it?" Mentor asked.

"Door. Wooden by the feel of it," said Odysseus.

"Will it open?" Helen asked.

"*Should* we open it?" Penelope asked.

Odysseus felt along the door until his hands came to a metal ring. He twisted it to the left, then to the right. At the second twist, the door made a noise somewhere between a click and a sigh, and opened forward, flooding the tunnel with light.

None of them stepped through. They just gathered at the door's edge and stared in.

There was an enormous room spread out before them. Oil lamps atop tripods in each corner flickered with warm light.

Odysseus was impressed. "This room's as large as my father's banqueting hall."

"A banqueting hall without couches or chairs?" Helen's voice was full of disdain.

The room contained a dozen long benches and wooden tables on which rested an assortment of hammers, hasps, pincers, and other instruments, as if the user had just stepped away for a moment.

Helen gasped. "Magic!"

"Don't be silly," Penelope told her. "It's a workshop."

But Mentor was the only one looking beyond the implements. "There's the master," he whispered, pointing to a white-robed man in an alcove to the right side of the room.

"And is that his wife?" Penelope asked, equally softly.

A few feet farther was another alcove, occupied by a beautiful young woman. *More beautiful, in a way,* Odysseus thought, *than Helen.*

He wondered what Mentor would think of that!

Or Helen.

When the master didn't immediately summon them

into the workshop, Odysseus went forward, followed quickly by the others, holding his hands out, palms upward, in a gesture of friendship.

"We're shipwrecked and far from home," he told the white-robed man. "May we have your help?"

Neither the master nor his lovely wife made any response.

"They're not moving," Penelope whispered.

"I don't think they're even breathing," Odysseus said. He walked up to the man and touched his face. The cheek was marble.

Astonished, Odysseus said, "Statues!" He examined the young master closely, marveling at the details. "Look how lifelike they are."

The four of them crowded around the statue of the young man, then they turned to look at the young woman.

"Who but Daedalus could have made them?" Penelope said. "This *has* to be his workshop."

Odysseus turned around to look over the workshop more carefully. Built into one wall was a kiln with a forge close by. Small jointed figurines of people and animals fashioned from wood and plaster were arranged on many of the shelves. Whoever Daedalus was, he was a master at his work.

"What use is all this?" Helen complained. "We need food, water, couches, servants." She plucked unhappily at the folds of her dress. "And a change of clothes."

"Surely we'll find something useful here," Penelope

said soothingly. "There should be another room, where Daedalus could sleep and eat." She started to look around for a door.

"What's this—a guard dog?" Mentor stood by the side of a metal hound, its body formed of bronze plates riveted together. For eyes it had a pair of rubies that glittered in the flickering light.

Helen laughed. "Woof! That dog couldn't scare anyone."

Mentor smiled. "Certainly not me." He spotted a nearby chest and started toward it. "What about this, Odysseus? Maybe there's clothing in it we can borrow?"

Odysseus joined him.

A strange clanking began. Then a muted metal growl.

"Stop!" Odysseus whispered hoarsely, putting his hand on Mentor's shoulder. "Don't move."

Mentor halted in midstride.

The bronze dog's jointed legs moved forward awkwardly, and its head turned with the noise of two metal plates scraping together. The jaws opened, exposing twin rows of sharp metal teeth. Then the jaws clanged shut, sounding like a sword being slammed back into its scabbard.

"Back away slowly," Odysseus whispered. "Hands out. Show the dog we're leaving the chest alone."

They edged backward, but the jeweled eyes followed them.

"Don't move!" Penelope cried out. "It fixes on motion!"

At her voice, the dog's head swiveled toward her.

The moment the dog looked away, Odysseus and Mentor each took another step backward.

The great head heard them and swiveled back.

"It fixes on sound, too," whispered Mentor.

Suddenly, with an awful grinding noise, the dog bounded forward, knocking Odysseus aside and ramming Mentor in the belly. Then it skidded to a halt and waited until Mentor—staggering—began to rise.

The bronze dog moved stiff-legged toward him, clashing its terrible teeth as it advanced.

Now behind the dog, Odysseus thought frantically. The knife would be useless against the metal dog. The satyr's club would have to do. He pulled it from his belt.

"Here," he cried, "over here, hound." He banged the club twice on the workshop floor to get the creature's attention.

The bronze dog turned toward him, then charged. Odysseus brought the club down on the dog's skull with all of his might.

The metal rang like a gong, and the club broke cleanly in two.

"Oh, oh!" Odysseus cried, and without thinking, jumped aside.

The dog looked up, swiveled its head till it found Odysseus again, and grinned its metal grin.

Then it started after him.

CHAPTER SEVENTEEN

A BOX FULL
OF MARVELS

"**R**un, Odysseus!" Penelope cried.

The dog turned its head toward the sound of her voice, and in that instant Odysseus vaulted over the nearest workbench.

Swiveling back, the dog found Odysseus at the height of his vault and leaped over the bench after him.

Odysseus ducked low, and one of the metal paws scraped his hair as it landed behind him.

A clay jar broke on its back, and this distracted the dog for a moment, long enough for Odysseus to roll under the table and get to the other side. He saw Penelope hoisting another jar to throw.

"No!" he yelled. "It will come after you!"

Penelope glanced behind her, where Helen stood

trembling. She made no move to throw the second jar.

Meanwhile Odysseus was running again, the hound right behind him, knocking over tables and benches. As he ran, Odysseus looked for anything resembling a weapon, but there was nothing there but pincers and hammers and . . .

He grabbed up a hammer as he passed one table, turned briefly, and tossed it over his shoulder at the bronze monster as hard as he could. The hammer bounced off the dog's snout and—for a second—it was confused. Then it went after Odysseus once more.

Odysseus had been watching over his shoulder and so did not see the stool in his way. He tripped and fell over it, executing a quick roll. But before he could get up, the hound had bounded forward, trapping him in a corner.

The bronze maw creaked open.

Odysseus could count many—too many—teeth. *Is this it?* he thought. *To die without landing a serious blow? To die lying on the floor of a . . . a workshop?*

"Odysseus!" called Mentor.

The dog looked toward the voice as Mentor snatched one of the wooden figurines from its shelf, then tossed it toward Odysseus. The figurine arced through the air, and the dog reared up to snatch it.

But Odysseus stood quickly and leaped higher, catching the figurine in both hands, and in a single fluid motion he thrust it lengthwise into the dog's gaping mouth.

The beast pounced, pinning Odysseus to the floor, but this time when its jaws snapped shut, the sharpened teeth sank deep into the wooden figurine. It growled and rumbled and clanked. The hinges of its jaw strained and squeaked. But its teeth were jammed fast.

Odysseus didn't let go of the wooden figure, and he was yanked helplessly from side to side as the dog jerked its head back and forth in an effort to free itself.

"Stop it!" Odysseus cried. "Stop it, you hairless, metal monstrosity."

But the dog didn't—or couldn't—stop. It continued to shake its head, and as it did, a harsh metallic grinding inside the dog rose higher and higher in pitch till it reached an earsplitting whine.

Snatching up hammers, Penelope and Mentor ran over to help, and now they began banging the bronze dog on the head.

"The eyes," Odysseus shouted. "Go for the eyes."

The hound shook its head harder and harder as first Mentor, then Penelope, cracked its jeweled eyes. The metal plates buckled under the strain. Rivets popped from the metal frame. One of the bronze legs broke free and clattered to the floor.

Mentor gave one more hammer blow at the right eye, and it popped out of its metal socket.

The bronze dog fell over, its remaining legs twitching spasmodically as its metal chest plates burst apart. Notched wheels and thin metal rods spilled out over the floor. The dog gave one final shudder, and—with an awful clank—fell silent.

"What a terrible thing to do to rubies," Helen commented.

Odysseus couldn't help himself. He began to laugh and laugh.

Penelope joined him.

Even Mentor began to giggle.

"Well, it *is*," Helen said.

With that, they all simply rolled on the floor, convulsed.

It took a while before they could stop laughing. But at last Odysseus sat up and poked the dog with his foot.

A few more wheels fell out of its chest.

"If I ever meet Master Daedalus . . ." he began.

"He's long in his grave," Mentor said. "If you'd listened to that bard . . ."

But Odysseus was already walking across the room to the chest that the dog had been guarding. "Let's see what manner of treasure that beast was keeping safe." He didn't tell them that walking helped him control the shakes. His legs were twitching just as the bronze dog's had. Odysseus refused to believe it was fear that made his legs tremble. After all, what was there to be afraid of now?

He lifted the lid of the chest. What he saw inside was the last thing he'd expected to see.

The chest was filled with thin sheets of pale leaflike material inscribed with drawings and symbols.

"Script," he said disgustedly. "Nothing but script. Penelope—can you read this?"

She got up, came over, and took the papyrus from his hands. Spreading the sheets out over one of the long tables, she pored over them for many minutes. Finally she looked up.

"Well?" Odysseus asked.

"I can read some of it. I've watched my father's scribes enough," she said. "Here's Daedalus' name again." She pointed to the bottom of one page.

Odysseus took the golden key out of his tunic and compared the two groups of signs. "I can see that," he growled. "What else?"

Penelope frowned and looked down again at the papyrus. "It's full of long, complicated words I've never heard of before. Things like *high-draw-lick*. And *awe-toe-mat-ick*."

Mentor sat down next to her. "Where does it say that?"

She showed him the script on the page. "I think these are instructions for making things, because there are drawings of many strange things, too." She pointed out a tall, pointed building, a strange-looking chair with legs like a woman's, water flowing down a series of complicated channels, a pair of wings, a plated hound.

"That's the dog we just fought," Helen said.

No one argued with her use of "we."

"And there's the ship," Odysseus said, picking up four of the sheets on which both the outside and the inside of the ship were drawn. The inside drawings showed clearly how the wheels and rods fitted together to make the oars work. There was also a lot of script on the page, which meant nothing to him now. He stuffed the papyrus down the front of his tunic and promised himself that when he got back to Ithaca, he would learn how to read it.

When.

Not *if*.

Just then Helen—who'd been unaccountably and blessedly silent—gave an awful yelp and tumbled to the floor. A marble plinth that she'd sat down on was even now sinking into the floor.

"Is this another of Daedalus' tricks?" she cried.

Before anyone could respond, there was a thunderous rumbling from somewhere above their heads.

"A storm?" Penelope asked.

Odysseus' eyes narrowed; his mouth went dry. A prickling at the back of his neck warned him that something much more serious was about to befall them, only he didn't know what.

The thundering sound was closer now.

And louder.

The room began to shake.

Suddenly, with an awful certainty, Odysseus knew.

"Get out!" he cried, pushing the others toward the

door. "Out! Out! Out!"

Penelope grabbed Helen by the arm and dragged her through the door, down the dark passage toward the great bronze door, which was still agape.

As they got closer, a huge boulder crashed down in front of the opening and rolled away toward the stone jetty.

"By the Furies!" Mentor gasped. "Are the gods playing skittles with us?"

"Not the gods," Odysseus cried. "Daedalus." He took a deep breath. "We've got to get out of here right now!"

More boulders rolled down from the cliffs above them.

"If we go out, we'll be crushed," Penelope shouted back.

"If we get pinned inside here, we'll be buried alive," he replied, charging outside.

The others followed, but they looked up fearfully. The entire cliff face was breaking apart above them, sending torrents of stones large and small tumbling down toward the harbor.

"The tunnel," Helen screamed. "We'll be safe there." She lifted her skirts and began running straight toward the sea cave. But as she ran, one of her sandal straps broke, and she fell, sprawling, some twenty steps short of her goal.

"Helen!" Mentor cried. Without hesitating, he scooped her up in his arms and ran with her toward the cave. As he ran, a small stone glanced off his ear and a larger one grazed his back, but he kept to his feet.

Right behind him came Penelope, and then Odysseus. At the last minute, Odysseus turned and looked back at the ship.

Huge rocks the size of horses were raining down on it, splintering the decks.

"Nooooo," he moaned as the hull buckled and cracked.

Then Penelope grabbed him by the arm and yanked him into the sea cave just as a boulder the size of the bronze hound hit the ground where he'd been standing.

He touched his tunic, where the papyrus drawings were stowed. *If it takes me years,* he thought, *I'll build another such ship, greater than the* Argo *my father sailed on.* And, he promised himself, he'd make a voyage such as no man had ever made before.

"I swear this by the gods," he whispered.

Only Penelope heard, and she didn't ask him what it was he swore. It was as if she already knew.

CHAPTER EIGHTEEN

RITES FOR THE DEAD

While they huddled ankle-deep in water, the rocks outside the tunnel piled up until they were all but blocking the tunnel mouth. The walls vibrated with the impact of stone upon stone.

"We need to get out of here before the roof collapses," Odysseus said, starting to slog through toward the open end.

Mentor agreed. "Lucky the tide's going out, or we could have been drowned."

The girls followed right behind them, though Helen limped slightly because of her missing sandal.

When they emerged out the other side, they all blinked in the sudden light.

"Dry land and daylight," Helen said, pointing to a

shingle of sand. "Things are looking better." She stumbled toward the sand.

Penelope and Mentor cried out together, "Helen, no!" Odysseus reached for his dagger.

Out of the woods above the beach a dozen armed men suddenly appeared, striding toward them. Four held spears, three mighty bows with the arrows already nocked; the rest had drawn swords.

Odysseus took his hand away from the knife. *A boy with a knife,* he reasoned to himself, *is no match for fully armed men.* He brought his hand up weaponless. *Better to use my brain.*

"We come in peace!" he cried.

One young man, in bright bronze armor and a high-crested helmet, strode ahead of the others. He had a fierce hawk face.

When he got close to them, he laughed and called over his shoulder, "Stand easy, men. These are only children." He was scarcely older himself.

Odysseus bristled. *I'm no child,* he thought. *I'm a prince of Ithaca, old enough to have already slain a boar, rescued two princesses from pirates, and beaten a bronze hound.* But he didn't say it aloud.

One of the swordsmen, gray-bearded, with corded muscles and a deep scar over his right eye, stepped between them. He held his sword chest-high and pointed right at Odysseus' throat.

"Idomeneus, my prince," he said in a gravelly voice,

"in this place who knows what form an enemy may take. Remember that young Theseus, who slew the beast in the maze, was but a boy. Remember the trickery of Daedalus and his little son."

"You worry too much, Bosander," said the prince. He took off his helmet and wiped his sweating face with the back of his hand.

The older man didn't lower his sword and, once again, Odysseus' fingers went to the hilt of his dagger, which he pulled out slowly, insolently.

"Hsst," Penelope said in his ear, "what are you thinking? One knife against a dozen armed men? You'll just get us all killed."

Odysseus knew she was right. But he'd already figured that out on his own. He hated that she didn't trust him.

Bosander knocked the knife from Odysseus' unresisting fingers with his sword.

"I was just giving it to you, old man," Odysseus said. "No need to stand a sword's length away."

Bosander moved close and pulled at the thong around Odysseus' neck with more roughness than was necessary.

A gasp went through the men.

"Look, my lord!" one cried.

Idomeneus stiffened. "Take it, Bosander!"

The gray-bearded soldier sliced the thong with his sword and, dropping the bronze spearhead on the sand, kept the golden key.

"Are you brigands waiting to rob us when we have done you no harm?" Odysseus demanded, his voice hotter than his heart.

Idomeneus glowered at him. "Mind your tongue, stripling!" he warned. "Though you're an Achaean by your speech, you're still a stranger here. Be careful how you address the son of Deucalion, king of Crete."

Glowering in silence, Odysseus knelt and picked up his humble amulet, tying it around his neck once more.

Bosander handed the gold key to Idomeneus. "This is surely the key the man Praxios spoke of, my prince. He didn't lie."

"Few men lie when faced with the threat of the Labyrinth," the prince remarked slowly. His eyes grew hooded, the lids closing halfway down. He took a step closer to Odysseus, looking more like a hawk than ever. "How did you come by this key, boy?"

Odysseus shrugged the insult away, but a deep line grew between his eyes. "It was just lying there in the sea cave. I almost missed it in the dark. But my foot connected with it, and it rang out against the stone wall. Never leave gold lying about, I say."

"What were you doing in the cave?" Bosander asked.

"We took shelter from a storm and rock slide," Odysseus replied innocently. "When we emerged, there you were, waiting for us. Not much of a reception for *children* in this Crete of yours."

Idomeneus eyed the others. "We had no storm on

this side. And *whose* children are you?"

Ever mindful of his grandfather's warning that knowledge was a two-edged weapon, Odysseus was about to begin a false story. But Helen stepped in front of him.

"I am Helen, princess of Sparta, captured by pirates and escaped here by the grace of the gods. I demand in the name of my father King Tyndareus that you treat me with the respect proper to my station. And my handmaiden Penelope as well."

Odysseus cursed silently, but Idomeneus seemed impressed.

Even more than impressed.

Struck down like Mentor, possibly unmanned.

Which may be to our advantage, Odysseus thought. He kept silent and watched the Cretan prince.

Idomeneus bowed. "Despite the dirt and the worn clothes, I can well believe you're a princess. But alas, Helen of Sparta, at the moment I have little hospitality to offer you." He turned back to Bosander. "Watch them all while I go into that cave."

Key in hand, he headed into the sea cave. A moment later he was out again, roaring. He brandished the key in Odysseus' face. "What's happened here?"

"I don't know," Odysseus said, keeping his voice guileless, though the crease between his eyes deepened. "We took shelter in the cave, and suddenly there was a sound of rocks falling, and the walls began to shake. We ran this way, afraid of being buried alive."

"And you saw nothing of what lies beyond?" demanded Idomeneus.

Odysseus shook his head.

Idomeneus turned to Helen. "Is this true, princess?" His eyes narrowed. "If you truly *are* a princess."

"*If* I'm a princess?" Helen's voice rose with her indignation. "When you insult me this way, what reason have I to answer?"

She folded her arms and looked at him from under a fringe of hair. It was the kind of look that could bring strong men to their knees, and Idomeneus was young enough to be smitten. But Odysseus thought he detected a false note in Helen's voice. Suddenly he realized that Helen was playacting.

Thank you, he whispered under his breath. It would buy them some time. Time, he knew, was always on the side of the prisoner.

"I meant no insult, princess. But I must know *everything* about this key. See—it's marked with the name of the traitor, Daedalus. Everything of his interests us. We shall return to the city and see what my father has to say." He put a hand on Helen's arm. "You come with me, Helen of Sparta. As for the others . . ." He turned to Bosander.

"Bring them all along," Bosander suggested.

Idomeneus nodded. His men jumped to do his bidding, and Odysseus, Penelope, and Mentor were suddenly and ably surrounded and taken in hand.

〓〓〓

They marched back into the woods and along a well-worn trail. Helen's sandalless foot was bound up by Idomeneus with a piece of cloth ripped from his own tunic.

The trail led across rugged foothills to a plain where twenty chariots waited, guarded by armed men. The Cretan horses were small, black, and well muscled, with slim heads and eager legs.

"Back to the city," Bosander commanded.

The four were not treated roughly, but separated and placed in different chariots. At a signal from the prince, the charioteers slapped their reins against the horses' rumps, and the little horses began to pull.

Odysseus was impressed with how smoothly the Cretan horses ran, galloping in quick, short bursts of speed. He said so to the charioteer, who glanced briefly over a shoulder at him.

"Specially bred. We keep brothers together. The king is a horse lover. So is his son." The charioteer spoke in short bursts, too.

"My father loves horses. Poseidon, bull roarer, keeper of the horses of the sea, has special shrines on our land," Odysseus told him. Not a lie exactly. But not all of the truth.

"Ah, the king will like that," the charioteer said, and turned back to his task.

Odysseus smiled. He'd learned more than he'd told. Always a good thing to do when in the company of enemies.

The sun was beginning to sink when the chariots turned east and traveled along a rough track by the coast. The sea here was a deep green, and the waves rolled in, high-crested, fierce.

They rode past a particularly jagged piece of the coast, where rocks like teeth pointed out at the sea.

Suddenly something in the fading light caught Odysseus' eye: a ship impaled upon the outer rocks, hull smashed beyond repair. The white-and-red eye on the side of the ship seemed familiar.

Captain Tros' ship!

"My lord Idomeneus, wait!" Odysseus cried out.

Hearing him, Helen pulled at the prince's shoulder. He signaled to his men, and soon they'd all reined in their horses.

Idomeneus got down from the chariot and walked over to Odysseus. "Why have you stopped us, boy?"

"That ship—" Odysseus began.

"Sea raiders," Idomeneus said. "Come to steal from us."

"But . . ." Mentor shut up when he saw the look on Odysseus' face.

"The very ones who kidnapped Princess Helen, her handmaiden, and us, great prince," Odysseus said. "Are they all dead?"

Bosander grunted. "Some." He pointed to five bodies lying several hundred yards away. "The rest we've taken to be sold as slaves."

"Unburied . . ." Mentor said.

Again Odysseus shut him up with a look. As the dead sailors' prince, Odysseus knew he was responsible for the men, though he'd had nothing to do with them for many days. Still they needed a proper burial, or else their shades could not cross over and enter the land of the dead. He would have to trick Idomeneus somehow.

He thought quickly, then said, "Great prince, I'm Epicles of Rhodes, and we guard our realm as fiercely as you do yours. But we believe that no matter what a person has done to us, we must show the same respect to the unburied dead as we would to a stranger seeking sanctuary at our door."

"When a *thief* comes to my door, I don't entertain him," Idomeneus retorted.

"But all who sail the sea are sacred to Poseidon," Odysseus said. He gestured up the beach where the unburied sailors lay. "To treat them this way dishonors the bull roarer himself."

Idomeneus' hawk face turned a deep russet color. "Do you, a mere boy, a Rhodian, dare speak to me of my duty to the gods?"

Shrugging casually, Odysseus said in placating tones, which still carried to all of the soldiers, "I only speak what I know, great prince. And to spare your land the fate that once befell mine." The deep line appeared between his eyes.

"What fate?" Bosander asked.

"When my king, Lord Tlepolemos, first came to Rhodes, he found a land ravaged by famine and plague. The dead were piled high in the streets; children wept because of empty bellies. Brave Tlepolemos, son of mighty Hercules, discovered the reason." He hesitated, waiting for the question to come. As he knew it would.

"What reason?" called out a soldier.

"Yes, tell us," cried another.

Idomeneus sighed. "Go ahead, boy. Finish your tale."

"Great Idomeneus, it's a story carved from history, as true as . . . as this Rhodian teller." He gazed wide-eyed at the prince with what he hoped looked like innocence. "Tlepolemos found a hidden bay where many ships had been swept onto the rocks. There, unburied, lay the remains of a hundred sailors. For this sacrilege Poseidon had cursed our island."

"And . . ." Prince Idomeneus said, clearly tired of the story.

"And the brave Tlepolemos buried every one of those dead seamen himself in a single night, a feat worthy of his father. From that day till this, Rhodes has been free of Poseidon's curse and has prospered under Tlepolemos' wise rule."

The Cretan soldiers and charioteers were silent for a moment. Then they began to move restlessly, even fearfully.

Finally one man dared the question they all wanted to ask.

"Brave Idomeneus, shouldn't the dead men be buried?"

Bosander spoke for the prince. "You, Epicles, and your friend—whatever his name is—can bury the dead yourselves. In a single night. Like your noble king."

The prince smiled slowly. It made his hawk face even fiercer. "Yes—it's only right that you two *invaders* work for your suppers."

As they dug the five graves in the sandy soil, well above the high tide mark, Odysseus was silent, but Mentor complained continually.

"One shovel between us? And the stink? And to do this on an empty belly? I'm not a son of Hercules. Nor are you . . ."

At last his rote of misery drove their Cretan guards back to the campfires, which left the two boys alone with their awful task.

The minute the guards were gone, Mentor turned to Odysseus. Holding up sandy hands, he said, "What were you thinking—telling all those lies? *Epicles of Rhodes!*"

"Keep digging," Odysseus whispered.

Mentor bent down and dug some more with his hands, looking like some sort of hound at work burying a bone. "Why not tell them the truth?" He looked up over his shoulder.

Odysseus smiled slyly. "The truth, Mentor? And what would you have me say? That these were *my* men? My grandfather's men? We would be dead on the sand next to them."

Mentor was silent.

Odysseus continued. "There are three reasons to lie to the Cretans. First, it gives us power over them, for we know what they don't. Second, it buys us time, the prisoners' only coin. And third—"

Mentor stood up and, hands on hips, interrupted. "And third, you just like to tell stories."

Ignoring his friend, Odysseus finished, "And third, it gets these good men buried." He dug into the fourth grave with pretended gusto. "So shut up and dig, Mentor."

Mentor returned to his digging. But after a bit he looked up again. "What were they doing here, so far from home?"

"Looking for us. Can you imagine Tros going to Father and saying, 'By the way, I lost your son overboard, Laertes.' Not and keep his head." He thrust the shovel into the sand.

"Was that story—the one about Rhodes—true?"

Leaning on the shovel, Odysseus grinned. "What do *you* think?"

Mentor shook his head. "I no longer know with you, Odysseus."

"Penelope does," Odysseus whispered. But Mentor had turned back to his digging and so he didn't hear.

Finally, sand-covered and with aching backs, the boys rolled the dead sailors into their graves and covered them over with sand.

Several of the soldiers had wandered over to watch. One gave Odysseus a piece of bread. Another loaned him a wineskin.

"Mighty Poseidon," Odysseus said, breaking the bread into crumbs, which he tossed into the air, "let these sailors who died on your wine-dark waters go swiftly into the land of the dead." He poured the wine into the sand as a further offering.

A third soldier grumbled, "Waste of good wine, that."

Odysseus ignored him and went on. "Father Zeus, hear our prayers." He raised his eyes to the full moon. "Send swift Hermes to guide these sailors to the distant west."

Looking around at the soldiers, Mentor added quickly, "And may their families be assured that even in a foreign land, they received a proper burial, one that is pleasing to the gods."

Bosander joined them. He said in a gruff but not unkind voice, "Wash off in the sea, boys. Then join your womenfolk at the fire. We've saved you a bit of food."

CHAPTER NINETEEN

THE GREAT KING'S PALACE

"*A bit* of food?" complained Mentor. "Hardly even a *bite*." He looked down at the wineskin and the half loaf of hard bread.

Odysseus wolfed down what they'd been given without measuring it.

"We'd hardly any more," Penelope told them. "Though Idomeneus did give Helen some dried dates."

Odysseus swiped his mouth with the back of his hand and glanced at their captors. Smiling, he waved at the nearest soldiers, who pointedly ignored him. "Soldiers on a scouting trip never carry great stores. We must be soldiers, too."

"Not I," Helen said, stretching prettily. "I'm a princess. When we get to the palace, there'll be kitchens and beds and baths and—"

"And dungeons," Mentor put in grimly.

"*And* the Labyrinth," Odysseus added, though he seemed almost excited at the prospect.

"What's Idomeneus been looking for?" Penelope asked.

"What we found," Odysseus said. "Daedalus' workshop. But we mustn't tell him that. Because then he'll find out we destroyed the place. And he won't be happy about that." He looked particularly at Helen as he spoke.

Helen shrugged prettily. "All I did was sit down on a plinth."

"I doubt Idomeneus will see it that way," Penelope told her. "And *I'll* be sure that he finds out whose fault it was."

"It was an accident," Helen began to wail.

Penelope shut her up with a quick elbow to the ribs. "Listen to Odysseus."

"We've got to go along with the Cretans for now," he said. "We're in no position to fight off or escape a band of armed warriors."

"Besides," Penelope added, "where would we go?"

"And what would we do for food?" Mentor added. "Dried bread will only get us so far."

"Exactly," Odysseus said. "We need a ship, food, weapons, and the rest of Tros' sailors if we're to make it off this island." He didn't tell them he'd no idea how to manage all that. *One thing at a time.*

Just then Idomeneus came over. "Better get to sleep," the prince said. "Soldiers rise very early. And we've still got a long ride in the morning. Princess Helen, are you comfortable?"

She dimpled at him. "I'll be more comfortable when we're at your palace," she said.

Comfort, Odysseus thought grimly, *is the enemy of the hero.* How often he'd heard that from his father's soldiers. Nevertheless, in his sleep he dreamed of hot food, sweet wine, and a soft bed.

In the morning, as early as Idomeneus had promised, they set off again along the dusty road, soon turning inland.

Well before noon they came to a small village with an inn the size of a pigsty, and as inviting.

Odysseus and Mentor now had their legs tied with just ropes, to ensure that they didn't wander. Odysseus suspected that it was Bosander who'd made that decision.

However, the innkeeper brought the girls water to wash in, as well as plates of cheese, olives, dates, and wine. A garrulous sort, the innkeeper exchanged pleasantries with the soldiers as well. He ignored the boys.

"Just as well," Odysseus whispered to Mentor. "I didn't understand a word he said anyway."

"I didn't want a conversation with him," Mentor said. "Just some of his food."

It was the charioteer who enlightened Odysseus as

they charged along the rock-strewn road. "The inn-keeper speaks Cretan. And badly. We"—he struck himself on the chest proudly—"we are Achaeans. We conquered this land."

No wonder Idomeneus and his men are so edgy, Odysseus thought. His father always said it took ten generations to conquer a people. From Minos to Deucalion to Idomeneus was a short three.

By afternoon, they were traveling along a broad, paved highway, wider and smoother than any Odysseus had ever seen. Along the roadside were shrines, stone markers inscribed with the image of a double-headed axe.

Soon they passed small villages made of white-washed stone houses; then two-story houses of brick began to crowd the roadside.

"Knossos," said the charioteer. "Our capital."

Odysseus watched carefully. If they were to escape, they'd have to know the way.

The outskirts of Knossos were chockablock with airy dwellings, noisy workshops, long storage barns. To the north Odysseus could see a wide harbor where ships bobbed at anchor. But the chariots didn't turn in that direction. Instead they passed through a pair of enormous gates into the city itself.

"The palace of Minos," said the charioteer, reining in the horses so that Odysseus could have a better look.

Odysseus stared, amazed. The Cretan palace was

twice the size, ten times the size—no, twenty times the size—of his father's and his grandfather's palaces combined. It seemed to stretch away as far as he could see, story upon story rising up on thick russet pillars. Unlike the palaces he knew at home, kept within high defensive walls, this structure sprawled outward in every direction, as if the makers had no fear of intruders. Workshops, stables, storerooms had accreted to the central building, making the place enormous. To the south and west were bright yellow-walled apartments looking like honey spilling from a jar.

Without wanting to, Odysseus found himself awed. But he bit his lower lip to keep from giving himself away.

The chariots halted at last, before a high stone gateway carved with the double axe. Idomeneus and his men dismounted and, herding their prisoners along, entered a pillared courtyard.

"This is . . . incredible," Mentor whispered to Odysseus. He kept swiveling around to see what lay on every side. "Can the gods on Olympus have anything this magnificent?"

Helen, too, was amazed. "What riches. What power . . ."

"Look over there," Odysseus whispered to them. "Those walls on the left side. See—they've been blackened with fire, and not recently either, I'd guess. And I saw some ruined houses on the western edge that haven't been repaired."

Penelope nodded. "I see what you're getting at,

Odysseus. For all their riches and power, they've had a share of disaster, too."

"And not enough resources to fix it up." Mentor was thoughtful. "What do you think it all means?"

"I don't know," Odysseus said.

Idomeneus dismissed most of his men, including Bosander, but kept half a dozen as escort.

And as guard, thought Odysseus.

"The watchmen will have informed my father of my return," the prince said to his prisoners. "I'll take you before him and let him pass judgment."

Helen raised a quizzical eyebrow. "I don't know that I care to be judged." Then she smiled at him.

For a brief moment Idomeneus looked uncomfortable. Helen seemed to have that effect on a lot of men. Odysseus turned his face away, determined not to laugh, though it was difficult.

"Well . . . not you, princess," Idomeneus said haltingly. "But them. *They* need to be judged." He pointed at the boys, drew a deep breath, then said with rescued authority, "Come with me."

They followed him down a passageway, the guards at their heels. On one wall a huge painted bull frowned down on them. Then the passage opened up into a courtyard so vast, it was like the market square of a large city. Musicians strolled by playing lutes and flutes. Servants scurried about with trays of fruit. Men in colorful robes and ladies with painted faces sat on stone benches, chatting.

"Look!" Penelope whispered, and with her chin gestured upward.

Above them were tier upon tier of balconies, from which even more people stared down at them.

Idomeneus led them up a wide stair to a doorway. To one side loomed a statue of a beautiful woman who had snakes twining around her body. Two savage lions lay down at her feet like pet dogs.

Startled by the figure, Helen put a hand to her mouth.

"Don't fear, princess," Idomeneus said, moving close to her. "That's Britomartis, goddess of our island, who protects us from fire and flood."

"Only some of the time," Odysseus whispered to Penelope and Mentor. "The rest of the time their houses burn like anyone else's."

Then they entered the west wing, where sunlight slanted through windows and the dark corners were lit with lamps.

The floors were colorful mosaics: scenes of dolphins, fish, and bearded Poseidon with his great trident held aloft. Crossing the mosaics, Idomeneus led them into new passageways, which twisted and turned as though designed to baffle visitors.

"How do you find your way through this place?" Mentor mused aloud, but none of the guards answered.

At last they entered an antechamber, and Idomeneus ordered them to be silent.

A man who was clearly a court official stood by the door. He wore a formal white robe that stretched down to his feet, and his left wrist was weighted down by a strand of carved gemstones.

Sealing stones, Odysseus thought. His father used the same to mark the containers in which their stores were kept, though these looked much more elaborate.

"Prince Idomeneus, your father awaits you," the robed man said, bowing low.

Odysseus wondered what kind of a man King Deucalion was. Was he, like his father Minos before him, a man of war who sent foreigners to their deaths in the Labyrinth? Or would he treat them fairly? Should Odysseus admit to being a prince himself? Or should he keep that information secret still? He fidgeted, tapping his fingers against his thighs.

"Waiting," Penelope whispered to him, "is clearly not what you're good at."

"Waiting is a woman's gift," he whispered back.

Just then the door opened, and they were ushered inside.

The room was small given the size of the rest of the palace, but it was still impressive. The walls had been painted to resemble a forest inhabited by gryphons, with their lion bodies and eagle heads. Two of them stood rampant on either side of the great throne.

And there was Deucalion, almost dwarfed by his long purple robe. A jeweled crown sat on his head, and he held an ivory scepter in his right hand. His hair and beard were set in elaborate curls. Yet somehow he—like the room—was smaller than Odysseus had expected.

Deucalion leaned toward them, gray eyes as hooded as his son's. "Step forward," he said in a voice that was flint-hard. "And give me one reason why I shouldn't kill you."

CHAPTER TWENTY

THE GREAT KING'S DUNGEON

entor was the first to reply. Spreading his hands palm upward, he said, "We have committed no crime, my lord, other than being lost and helpless. My father always says that treating strangers badly offends mighty Zeus."

The king still leaned forward. "Zeus himself spoke to *my* father, boy, and gave him the laws by which our people are governed," he said. "The right of judgment has been passed down to me. I ask again: Give me one reason why I shouldn't kill you?"

This time Penelope spoke. "Because a king who is not fair is not wise."

Deucalion smiled and leaned back on his throne, but the smile didn't reach his eyes. "I'll judge you fairly enough, young lady. You are foreigners, which means you're probably spies. In all likelihood you've come here to prepare the way for an attack by your countrymen of . . ."

"Sparta," said Idomeneus.

"And Rhodes," added Odysseus. He'd held back his real name and lineage while assessing the king, thinking perhaps to confess it later. But now that he'd seen and heard the king, he was glad he'd kept quiet. King Deucalion had cruel eyes and a bitter voice.

"All Rhodians are liars," Deucalion stated. He shook the golden key at Odysseus. "Where did you get this?"

"I found it in the sea cave," Odysseus replied. "The others—who had gone ahead of me—knew nothing about it. I was keeping it for myself because of the gold."

"The gold!" Deucalion repeated contemptuously. "This small amount of gold is nothing compared to the treasures it might unlock." He leaned forward again and shoved the key toward Odysseus. "Can you read the inscription?"

Odysseus shrugged. "In Rhodes only hired scribes read. Real men—warriors and princes—don't bother."

"Daedalus' name is written here," said the king. "My father's craftsman. He promised to build my father a ship that needed neither wind nor oarsmen. For years I've been seeking that ship and Daedalus' secret workshop.

You swear you know nothing of this?"

"A magical ship?" Odysseus furrowed his brow, which made the vertical line between his eyes look deep as a wound. "Your majesty, if we'd found such a ship, would we be *here*?" He looked at his friends, and they all nodded solemnly. "Why not ask this Daedalus?"

Deucalion ground his teeth in anger. "Daedalus fled this island on magical wings. He caused my father's death. If he still lives, he's well beyond my wrath." The king rose from his throne and clenched the key tightly in his right hand. "Do you deny you are cohorts of Praxios, the one who robbed me of my prize?"

"I thought, sir, his name was Daedalus," Odysseus said. He kept his voice calm, though he could feel a little tic start in the corner of his eye.

The king's gray eyes were now the color of stone. "Praxios was his assistant."

"I swear by all the gods that I don't know this man," said Odysseus.

Deucalion turned to the others. "Do you all say the same?"

Mentor swallowed hard and shook his head. "I've never met anyone of that name, sire."

Penelope met the king's gaze in silence.

Helen turned pale but managed to shake her head.

Odysseus knelt. "Great king," he cried, "my companions' only offense is that they've been led by me. Keep the key by all means. Save any punishment for me alone."

"I would not be so ungenerous," said Deucalion. He signaled to the guards. "Take them all."

Idomeneus stepped quickly to Helen's side, and held up his hand, protecting her. "Father, please . . ."

Deucalion turned his stony eyes upon Helen. "Are you truly a princess of Sparta, as my son believes?"

Helen flushed and sniffed indignantly. "I'm the daughter of King Tyndareus. At this moment there are a thousand ships—"

Deucalion cut her off with a slicing hand gesture. He met his son's gaze. "Let her be taken to suitable apartments. We'll entertain her as a princess—for now."

Struggling against the soldiers' grip, Penelope cried out, "My lady cannot be expected to do without her faithful handmaiden."

Helen pulled herself from Idomeneus' hands. "I refuse to budge without my Penelope. She's both my handmaid and my cousin."

"Father . . ." Idomeneus appealed again.

There was a long moment of silence. Then Deucalion snorted through his nose like an irritated bull.

"Very well. But the other two go to the dungeon with Praxios."

Dragged roughly through yet another maze of passages, Odysseus and Mentor didn't even try to struggle free. But once they were pushed into the gloomy prison cell on the outskirts of the palace, Mentor turned on his friend.

"*Why*, Odysseus? Why say we're from Rhodes when the truth might have saved us?"

"And have my father pay tribute to that monster? I'd rather die," Odysseus retorted.

"You don't mean that," Mentor said.

"Oh yes, I do."

"We're *all* going to die here," came a sepulchral voice from a corner of the cell.

The boys turned. A wan shaft of light was poking through a grill in the ceiling, and by it they could just make out a filthy figure, long and lanky, like a wading bird. His head was shaved as bald as an egg, and his bright, beady eyes stared out at them from under bushy brows. A long gray beard, full of little pieces of yellow straw, came to a point in the middle of his chest.

"You must be Praxios," said Odysseus.

The man's eyebrows shot up like a pair of birds taking flight. "So my fame has traveled before me."

"The king mentioned you," said Mentor.

"Ah, the king." The bird-brows came to rest again.

"He doesn't seem to like you," Odysseus said.

"Well, as you're here too, I suspect he doesn't like you either," said Praxios. "Whoever you are."

"I'm Mentor," Mentor said. "And this is Odysseus, prince of—"

"Shut up!" Odysseus said with a growl.

"What does it matter here?" Mentor asked. "No point lying to him. He's a prisoner just like us."

"He could sell us to the king," said Odysseus.

"I could have sold out my master to the king long before this," said Praxios. "For a better cause." He stretched out his long, bony fingers. "That beast in human form threatened to crush my hands beneath a rock if I didn't tell him what he wanted to know: the secrets of my master, Daedalus."

Odysseus smiled. "You mean the workshop and the bronze dog and the hidden harbor?"

Praxios looked up sharply. "You've been there?"

"We ran into Prince Idomeneus nearby," Mentor said.

"Did he find his way in?" Praxios suddenly started shaking.

"No," Odysseus said, "the workshop was already buried under a mountain of rock."

Praxios gasped. "My master's final defense. I never had the nerve to use it myself."

Mentor said quickly, "It was set off by accident."

"And the ship?" Praxios was still shaking.

"Destroyed, too," Odysseus said. "By accident." There was a sharpness in his tone that made Mentor glance over at him.

"But I sent it far away," the old man said. "I'd heard from a friend that Deucalion's men were closing in on me. So I loaded the ship with supplies. I packed away the key and had just started the mechanism when they found me. One man climbed onboard and grabbed me as the ship moved away. We grappled and fell overboard, and the ship made off without me."

"We found the ship drifting at sea," Odysseus said. "Once we got aboard, I pulled the rod by accident, and the ship came to life. It carried us to Crete."

Praxios gave a dry laugh. "What a lot of accidents you boys seem to have!"

"No more than you, sir, to be toppled off your ship," said Mentor pleasantly.

"Ah—but you two started the self-winding mechanism that reversed the ship's course and brought it back to its starting point. Your accidents are happier than mine." Praxios nodded his head.

"Not so happy. They landed us in the same place as you," Odysseus pointed out.

For a moment they were all three silent, contemplating the dungeon.

At last Odysseus said, "Do you know how the ship works?"

"Not I. I'm a simple artisan. Only Daedalus could craft such a complex device. All I did was take care of it and the workshop in case my master should ever return to Crete. I considered that my life's duty, to keep the ship and workshop hidden from Minos' beastly son." Praxios stood and stretched. "Old bones. Can't lie around all day, like a vegetable in a field. Not even in a dungeon."

"Didn't Daedalus build the ship *for* King Minos?" Mentor asked.

"Oh yes. That he did. But once he realized Minos wanted a fleet of such ships in order to conquer the world, my master refused to say where the ship lay hidden. He managed to escape from Crete, but I—alas—did not."

Odysseus' hand strayed to the front of his tunic. He could feel the folded sheets of papyrus there, with Daedalus' plans for the construction of the ship. But he still was wary of the old man and said nothing.

"Well, now both ship and workshop are beyond this awful king," said Mentor. "So, old man, you can rest easy."

"*Easy?* How can I rest easy? I lie in a filthy dungeon, and every day I am taken out and beaten. One day they'll put me in the Labyrinth, and that will be the end of me," Praxios cried.

"The Labyrinth?" Odysseus whispered the word.

"And how can I rest when I don't know the fate of the golden key? You must have had that if you entered the workshop." Praxios' face took on a crafty look.

"Yes, we had the key. What does that matter?" Odysseus asked.

"The golden key is the master key," Praxios replied excitedly. "No one knows but I." He looked around as if fearing to be overheard.

"Master of what?" asked Mentor and Odysseus simultaneously.

"Maybe you're spies sent to catch me out," Praxios

suddenly whispered, crouching away from the boys.

"Let me tell you about the bronze hound," Odysseus said, leaning toward him.

"And the statues of the man and woman so lifelike they almost drew breath," added Mentor.

"Yes, yes—I see, you *have* been there. Give me the master key," Praxios begged.

"First," Odysseus said, leaning even closer, "tell us what else the key can master."

"Any lock made by the gods or men," the old man said, holding out a trembling hand. "That was one of the secrets foul Deucalion has never wrested from me."

"If only we still had the key," Mentor said, turning away.

"You don't have it?" Praxios cried, in a voice that sounded like a death rattle.

"Idomeneus took it from me," said Odysseus unhappily. "For all the good it is to us now, it might as well be on the other side of the ocean."

CHAPTER TWENTY-ONE

THE PROPHECY

here was no more to be gotten out of the old man. He simply rolled into a ball in his own corner and fell asleep, loudly snoring.

"I doubt the Minotaur itself made that much noise," Mentor complained.

The boys spent a miserable night on the cold stone floor. No matter how much straw they bunched under themselves, they couldn't get comfortable. Finally sheer fatigue put them to sleep.

When they woke in the morning—which they identified by the shaft of weak light coming through the ceiling grill—they were stiff all over. They could hear the sounds of the palace stirring to life.

Mentor sniffed loudly, trying to sort out any smells of food.

"Do we get breakfast?" he asked hopefully.

Praxios was already up and pacing around the small cell. "One meal a day," he said gloomily. "But at least it's always on time."

At midday a palace servant brought them a loaf of bread and a jug of brackish water. A burly guard stood in the open doorway watching them eat, his sword ready for any trouble. Once they were finished with the meager offerings, the guard took away the water jug, and the door was slammed and locked shut behind him.

As soon as he was gone, Odysseus began to search the cell, checking the walls, floor, corners, trying to find any way out of the place. He went around a second time. And then a third.

"There's not a loose brick or promising chink anywhere," he muttered.

Meanwhile Mentor was talking with old Praxios.

"So you learned to heat metal. And to shape it. But so can any smith," Mentor said.

Praxios shook his head. "Not like the master."

Mentor got very quiet. "Did he teach you any of his magic?"

Praxios laughed his dry little barking laugh again. "There was no *magic*."

As if the very word bid him, Odysseus stopped his

search and came over to them. "No magic? But what about the bronze dog? What about the ship? What about the . . . ?"

Praxios grinned. "No magic, boy. None. It was all craft. The master learned that motion can be stored just like grain or wine."

Odysseus snorted. "Store motion in a jar? That would be like keeping the wind in a bag."

"Not in a jar," Praxios said. He leaned forward and whispered, as if imparting a great secret. The boys both leaned in to hear. "It's contained in coiled lengths of metal."

"Metal!" This time Mentor laughed out loud.

But Odysseus was suddenly silent, listening.

"You wind the metal around itself again and again and keep it that way until you need the motion that's stored in it."

"That makes no sense at all," Mentor said. "Unless it's magic motion that's stored."

Praxios shook his head. "I don't understand any better than you do, but it works. You've seen it for yourselves."

Remembering the coiled metal in the bowels of the ship, the metal intestines spilling out of the bronze hound, Odysseus nodded.

Praxios suddenly shook all over. "But what does it matter?" he cried. "What does it matter? They're gone. All gone."

"Suppose . . ." Odysseus said quietly. "Suppose you had Daedalus' own plans. Could *you* build a new ship just like the one that's gone?"

Praxios rubbed his chin thoughtfully, which caused his thin beard to waggle. "Perhaps. It would take a lot of work, though. But I'm a good worker."

Putting a hand to his chest, feeling the crinkle of the parchment beneath his tunic, Odysseus was just about to confide his secret, when there was a sudden noise.

Hsst.

"A snake!" Praxios cried. "I hate snakes!" He scrambled into his corner.

"No, the sound came from up there," Mentor said, pointing to the grill above their heads.

"By all the gods," Odysseus whispered hoarsely, glancing up. "What are *you* doing here?"

"Helen!" Mentor cried. "Are you all right?"

Helen's hair had been elaborately arranged on top of her head with two long curls twining down over her cheeks. A row of pearls was strung across her brow, and a pair of gold earrings dangled from her ears. She'd been doused with perfume.

"You look so beautiful," Mentor whispered, transfixed by her.

For a moment she beamed at the compliment. Then she said, "I looked *beautiful* about an hour ago. But since then this new dress has gotten terribly soiled. I had to climb over a balcony and down a vine to get here. I shall have to take a bath when I get back to my apartment. You should see the bath. It's made out of a solid—"

Odysseus interrupted. "Why *are* you here?"

"It certainly isn't for the pleasure of *your* company," Helen said.

"If the king finds out, you're going to be in terrible trouble," Mentor began.

"*He's* the reason I've come," Helen said. "He's thrown Penelope into the Labyrinth. You've got to do something."

"Penelope!" Odysseus felt a shudder that began in his feet and worked its way up to the top of his head. His heart suddenly thudded in his chest. "But . . . but . . ."

"But *we're* supposed to be the ones punished," said Mentor.

"I know," Helen whispered. She looked around to make sure no one could see her. "It has to do with some silly prophecy. Something like 'When the maiden and the horned beast at—'"

Praxios corrected her. "'When maiden meets the horned beast at the heart of the Labyrinth, then will you find your heart's desire.'"

"That's it!" Helen cried, clapping her hands.

"It's something Daedalus told King Minos when he built the Labyrinth," Praxios said.

"I thought the Minotaur was dead," Odysseus said.

Praxios shrugged his bony shoulders. "King Minos never forgot those words. He said it was a prophecy. After my master escaped, even after the Minotaur was dead, the king continued sending foreign young maidens—boys, too—into the Labyrinth. He believed their sacrifice would give him his heart's desire and that the rule of Crete would go on forever."

"But Minos, too, died," Odysseus pointed out.

"His awful son rules," said Praxios. "The sacrifices continue. There are other monsters in the maze now."

"*Me,*" Helen said. "He was going to sacrifice *me!*" Her voice held a combination of horror and surprise. "But Idomeneus—may Aphrodite bless him—stood between me and the palace guards. He insisted they take Penelope instead."

"And you let them?" Odysseus asked.

For once she had the grace and wit to be silent.

"What could Helen have done?" Mentor argued. "Better one than two. And she's here now."

"Too little and too late," Odysseus said bitterly. "Penelope was worth twenty of you." He realized that he meant it.

Helen began to snuffle. "I know she is. I know. And I tried. I begged Idomeneus. I was still crying when he left me."

"Tears are not coins and buy little freedom," Odysseus said.

"I know. I know," Helen said. She wiped a hand across her nose, smearing the heavy Cretan makeup. "I ordered a servant to show me the way here. You should have seen him jump!" She gave a little hiccuping laugh. "I came so you can get out and rescue Penelope."

"Did you bring us swords?" asked Odysseus.

"Don't be silly! How could I carry swords?" Helen answered.

"A bow then?" Odysseus asked. "I'm really good with a bow."

"Of course not."

"Then how are we to get out?" Mentor asked.

"I thought clever Odysseus would have that figured out by now. I just came to be sure you went to rescue Penelope first," Helen said. "I guess he's not so clever after all."

Odysseus groaned.

"The key," old Praxios croaked.

"The key?" Mentor and Helen said together.

"The key!" Odysseus almost shouted, then remembered where they were. "Where is it? The golden key?"

"Why . . ." Helen looked puzzled. "In the treasury. Idomeneus took me there to pick out some jewelry and to put the key there."

"Can you find your way back to the treasury?" Odysseus said, trying hard to be patient and not succeeding.

"Of course," Helen said. "But it's very well guarded. You'll never get inside."

"*You*," he said, almost growling. "*You* will get inside, Helen."

"But why me? Haven't I already done enough?"

"You've been wonderful," said Mentor.

Odysseus kicked him on the shin. "You have to get inside *to get the key!*"

"Why that key?"

Honestly, Odysseus thought, *she is the dumbest girl in the entire world.* Then he remembered how she'd found her way to them. Maybe not *that* dumb. "Because the key is one of Daedalus' inventions. It will open any lock in Crete." He decided not to let her know it would open any lock in the entire world. Better not to give her too much information!

Helen tilted her head to one side, considering. "I'm not sure they'd let me in without Idomeneus."

"Order them to. Tell them you don't like the earrings you've got. Tell them you want to get a new pair," Odysseus said.

"You don't like the earrings?" Helen asked. "Are they too gaudy? I know they're too gaudy."

"It's just an *excuse*," Odysseus said, bristling with impatience. "I don't care about your earrings, so long as you get the key."

"Don't you take that tone with me, Prince Clever."

"Helen," Mentor said, his tone suddenly cozening, "we've got to get started at once if we're to save Penelope."

Helen stood. "All right. I'll try. You wait here till I get back."

She disappeared from the grill.

"As if we had somewhere else to go," Odysseus whispered.

CHAPTER TWENTY-TWO

HORNED BEAST

dysseus couldn't stop imagining Penelope wandering along the twisted tunnels of the Labyrinth.

Is she frightened? And then as quickly, *No, she'll be brave.*

But he knew that being brave, without weapon or friend to help, would not be enough.

Not against a beast in the dark.

He started pacing the cell restlessly. "Helen should have been back by now."

"Maybe she was caught," Mentor said.

"Maybe lost her nerve, you mean," Odysseus countered.

Mentor bit his lip. "You haven't given her enough time."

"How much time do you think *Penelope* has?" Odysseus said.

"Hush!" Praxios suddenly stood, finger to lip.

They shut up at once. There was a rustle above them, then a loud clink.

They looked up, then down. A gold key glinted in the straw.

"Now get on with it," Helen whispered, starting to move away.

"Wait," Odysseus called. "We need one more thing."

"I can't do any more. Idomeneus is probably already looking for me."

Mentor called, "*Please*, Helen. This and nothing more." He looked over at Odysseus.

Odysseus nodded. "Distract the guard, Helen. Or he'll cut us down as we try to leave."

"I thought you were a hero," she said.

"He *is* a hero," Mentor replied angrily. "He saved me from drowning, got us away from the pirates, fought the bronze dog and . . ." His voice ground to a halt.

Odysseus bit his lip. "Helen, we're two boys and"— he looked over at Praxios—"and a craftsman. The guard's a grown man with a sword. You figure it out."

"And how am *I* supposed to distract him? This grown man with a sword?"

"Just be yourself," Odysseus said.

Mentor kicked him in the shin.

Helen knelt again and whispered through the grate.

"If I do this, then everyone will know I helped you escape."

"Everyone will know anyway," Mentor said. "And in Sparta you'll be known for your bravery as well as your beauty."

"Do you want Penelope rescued or not?" Odysseus went to the heart of the matter.

"You'd better succeed, after all the trouble I've gone through," Helen said. Then she was gone.

They were silent until they heard the murmur of conversation in the outer hall where the guard stood watch. Trusting it was Helen—not just another guard—Odysseus slid the gold key into the cell door lock. He turned it gently until it give a satisfying *snick*, and the door opened.

"Sandals off," he whispered. Then, turning to Praxios, he took the old man's cloak.

They found themselves at the far end of a long corridor. Clear on the other side the burly guard hunched over, talking intensely with someone hidden from their view.

Their bare feet made no sound on the stone floor, and they crept up behind the guard until they could hear Helen's voice saying, "Should I turn left at the grain store?"

"No, mistress. *Right* at the store. Left at the *stables*." The guard spoke with the same irritation Odysseus did when talking to her.

"You've been"—she sighed loudly—"so helpful. And I've been such a silly goose." She put a delicate hand on his arm.

"No, mistress," he said, only this time he sounded as if her beauty had suddenly fuddled him.

It was then that Odysseus pounced, pulling the cloak over the guard's head and drawing it tightly around his thick neck while Mentor made a dive for the guard's legs.

The guard let out a bellow, which was muffled by the cloak, and kicked out before Mentor could reach him. He spun around, groping blindly for his sword. Odysseus was shaken this way and that, just as he'd been by the bronze dog. Only this time he lost his grip and tumbled across the floor.

Staggering across the passage, the guard was like a blinded beast. Helen kicked a little footstool in his way, and he tripped over it before he could rid himself of the cloak. Stumbling forward, he cracked his head on the wall and dropped senseless to the floor.

"Oh!" Helen cried. "I think I've broken my toe."

Odysseus scrambled over to the guard, drew the man's sword from the scabbard, and set it aside. Mentor hastened over as well. Only Praxios stayed back, huddled against the wall.

"He's still breathing," said Mentor.

"Use your belt to tie his hands behind his back," Odysseus said. "Then we'll lock him in the cell."

"Isn't anyone going to say thanks?" asked Helen.

The deed done, they hurried back up the stone corridor, only this time with their sandals on. Odysseus paused to pick up the heavy bronze sword. Mentor snatched a torch from the wall.

"Now, Helen, where's that Labyrinth?" Odysseus asked. He wished the sword were lighter. He would need two hands to wield it.

Helen shrugged and spread her hands helplessly.

"I know where the Labyrinth is," Praxios said. "Every Cretan knows. If only to avoid the place. It's close to the dungeon so they don't have far to transport prisoners."

They followed the old man out through three more sets of doors, then down a grassy slope, and between a pair of broken pillars. There a flight of wide stone steps led down into the earth, disappearing into darkness. Surprisingly they passed no one—guards or otherwise— along the way.

When Odysseus commented on that, Praxios shook his head. "Why should they bother guarding it?" he said. "Who goes in doesn't come out."

"It shouldn't be that hard to find the way back," Odysseus said. "We can make marks on the walls and follow them out."

"It's not that simple," Praxios told them. "Nothing the master ever did was simple. As soon as a person sets foot inside the Labyrinth, the whole thing changes."

"Changes?" Helen asked. Her face went bone white under the Cretan powder.

"The very walls shift position," Praxios said. He rubbed his hands together, as if in admiration of the craft.

"Then how did Theseus escape, with all the children of Athens?" Odysseus asked.

"Ah—Theseus. It's *always* Theseus," old Praxios said, his bird eyebrows fluttering. "The hero who escaped. I've never told the truth of it before, because we all need to believe in heroes, eh? Well, Theseus was not so much a hero, my children."

Odysseus' mouth turned down in a sour expression, but it was Mentor who asked, "If not a hero, then how did he escape?"

"Ah," said Praxios brightly, "the master jammed the mechanism for him. Theseus was from Athens and so was Daedalus, who had been a prince there once. And pretty little Ariadne, Minos' daughter, had fallen in love with Theseus. She was a particular pet of the Master's. He did it for her."

"I don't suppose you know the secret for jamming it yourself?" Odysseus asked. He put down the heavy sword for a moment, letting it rest against his leg.

Praxios lifted his hands apologetically. "The Labyrinth is as much a mystery to me as you. I was only a boy when it was built."

Odysseus looked down into the darkness and swallowed hard. He'd never told anyone, not even Mentor, but dark caves and tunnels made his stomach hurt. He preferred hunting monsters in the light.

Helen put a hand to her mouth. "We can't leave Penelope . . ." Her voice trembled. Her eyes teared up. The black makeup around her eyes ran down her cheeks in streaks.

"We're not leaving *anyone* down there," said Mentor.

"Especially Penelope," added Odysseus. He took a deep breath and lifted the sword again. His father once said that being brave was overcoming fear. *No fear,* he'd said, *no courage.* Odysseus admitted to himself that he was afraid.

No, he thought suddenly, *not afraid. Terrified.*

He put that thought aside. There was another problem that had to be dealt with as well.

"Praxios," Odysseus said, "where are the slave pens?"

"Down by the harbor," Praxios said. "So they can be loaded and unloaded quickly. We do quite a trade in slaves."

"Then," Odysseus said, "you three go on down to the harbor. See if you can find Tros and his men."

It was Mentor who guessed first. "You can't mean to go into the Labyrinth alone, Odysseus. That's crazy."

"No sense all of us going in," Odysseus said. If he was going to get weak-kneed in the cave, he certainly didn't want anyone else to see. Besides, this was a good plan. If he managed to free Penelope, they couldn't waste time trying to find the sailors and the boat. And if he didn't get her out . . . well, at least Mentor and Helen could get off the island. "You need to free Tros and find his ship to get us all away from here. Trust me—your job will be harder than mine."

Helen laid a hand on his arm. "Be careful, Odysseus."

There was something in her eyes he'd never seen before. A real concern for someone other than herself. It brought out her true beauty and, for the first time, he knew he was seeing her as Mentor did. As men would see her for years to come.

"Thank you," he said, and meant it.

Mentor handed him the torch silently. There were tears gathering in the corners of his eyes. Odysseus looked away before those tears called out his own.

Then he started down the steps, the heavy sword upraised in one hand, the flickering torch in the other. Halfway down he turned and looked back. Mentor was staring mournfully at him.

"Getting in is one thing," Mentor said. "But you heard Praxios. No one who's gone in has come—"

"I'll worry about that when it's time to leave. *With* Penelope," Odysseus said. "Now—go!"

This time Odysseus didn't look back. He continued down the stairs until reaching the bottom, where a long, black passage sloped underground. He rested the sword blade on his right shoulder and raised the torch.

"Athena, if you're ever going to help me, help me now."

Cautiously he advanced, step by step, remembering the Cretan prophecy: *When maiden meets the horned beast at the heart of the Labyrinth, then will you find your heart's desire.*

Just as he was pondering this, a huge block of stone crashed down behind him. The floor began to swivel. He realized that the entire passageway was revolving on some sort of axis.

Feeling seasick, his stomach lurching as the floor and walls moved on unseen rollers and wheels, Odysseus staggered a few feet forward, then steadied himself. Ahead were several long passages stretching away into darkness. Behind . . .

Behind, where there had been a passage, was a solid rock wall.

He held the torch up higher. There was nothing to indicate that any one way was better than any other, so he shrugged and set off at random, the sword against his shoulder even heavier than before.

The corridors bent to the left, then to the right, doubling back on themselves. Again and again Odysseus ran into dead ends, retraced his steps, only to feel the stone floor tip, roll, and change.

I'm being herded, he thought. *I'm being forced to choose a single path.* But there was nothing he could do about it. He went forward, he went backward, he went forward again.

Then ahead of him, he saw something humped up in the passageway. He held the sword out in front, the torch high, and ran forward. Anything to relieve the monotony of the place.

But he pulled up short when he saw what the hump really was: a human skeleton, its clothes shredded and stained with dried blood.

"Penelope," he whispered, even as he saw that the skeleton wore a man's tunic.

He stood very still, listening, the upraised sword trembling as his tired arm shook.

The Labyrinth was as silent as . . .

As a tomb.

"Not a good thought," he told himself, and moved on.

He found a second skeleton. Then a third. He thought they might be old. That the beast who had ravaged them might be old. Might even be dead.

He wondered if he should call out to Penelope. To let her know he was looking for her.

"Stupid idea," he whispered to himself. It would alert the beast.

He didn't want to alert the beast.

And then he heard a sound from ahead in the dark corridor.

Clip.

Clop.

Clip.

An animal's hooves on the stone floor.

Not dead, then, he thought. Meaning the beast. Hoping he meant Penelope. He set down the torch and moved out of its light.

It was easier holding the sword in two hands. Much easier.

He held his breath and went around a bend in the passage.

Clip.

Clop.

He raised his sword in both hands and waited, his palms sweaty. He hoped the beast could not smell him.

But he could smell the beast now: musky stink of a meat eater.

The hoofbeats came closer.

They were almost on top of him.

Releasing all his fear in one horrific battle cry, he leaped out of hiding and swung the sword.

A bulky figure reeled back, dropped a little light, and avoided the bronze blade by inches.

"Great Paaaaaan!" the old satyr exclaimed. "Is that any waaaay to greet aaaan old friend?"

CHAPTER TWENTY-THREE

LADON

Silenus picked up a bronze lamp from the Labyrinth floor. As he did so, the yellow flame cast flickering shadows over his little horns, making them look larger. For a moment he seemed as fearsome as any monster.

"*You're* the horned beast?" Odysseus cried.

"I don't know that I caaare for the term," Silenus said, "but thaaaat's whaaat the devil Deucalion caaaalled me."

Odysseus let the heavy blade touch the ground. His arm was now aching. "By all the gods, how did you get here?" He was so relieved to see the old satyr, he didn't even mind the stink.

"Those piraaaatical friends of yours were very persistent," Silenus said. "They finally caught me taaaaking

· 199 ·

a naaaap in my caaaave. They draaaagged me onboard aaaand brought me here, where the king bought me. A pretty price he paaaaid, too." There was a note of pride in his bleating voice. "A saaack full of gold aaaand jewels."

Suddenly remembering the skeletons, Odysseus said, "How long have you been here?"

"Two or three daaaays," Silenus answered uncertainly. "Deucalion supplied me with enough food to laaaast a week, or so he said. He underestimated my aaaappetite. It's gone, aaaand I've filled the lamp with the laaaast of the oil he left me."

"I have a torch," Odysseus said, gesturing behind him. "Back there. But it won't burn for long, either. Maybe we should just use one till the other is about to give out."

"Good plaaaan," the satyr said. "Do you have other plaaaans? You're very good with plaaaans." He smiled. It didn't improve his looks.

"My only plan was to kill the horned beast, rescue Penelope, and get out of here as fast as I could," said Odysseus.

Silenus nodded. "Good plaaaan," he said. "Except for the killing." He thought a minute. "Penelope is the pretty girl?"

"*I* think so," said Odysseus.

"I thought I smelled something. Aaaa flowery perfume. I hoped it was a haaaandmaid of the gods. That's where I was going now. Aaaa woman is better than food any daaaay. Though . . ." he sighed, "I could do with some food right now. Do you haaaave any?"

Odysseus shook his head.

"Well, then," said the satyr, "it will haaaave to be the girl. Get your torch. With my nose"—and he laid a finger against his nostril—"we'll find her soon enough."

As soon as Odysseus had retrieved his torch, they moved off smartly together. The sound of the satyr's hooves clippity-clopping kept echoing off the stone walls.

Every once in a while, Odysseus could feel the floors shift. Each time, when he turned around, the way behind was blocked. But as their journey went on, the shifts became fewer and fewer.

"We're getting close to the center of the maaaaze now," Silenus explained. "It's easier to find your waaaay. Nothing moves in the center."

"That's good," Odysseus said.

They came to an intersection, where Silenus paused for a few more sniffs. He nodded, turned right.

"Not faaaar," he said. "Yes—look!"

Ahead in the semidarkness, a burnt-out torch at her feet, a girl huddled against the wall. At the sound of Silenus' hooves, she stood, picked up the torch, and held it above her head like a cudgel. She was wearing a Cretan dress only slightly less splendid than Helen's, though spoiled from her time in the maze.

"You saaaaid she was the pretty one." Silenus' voice held disappointment.

Odysseus was so relieved to see Penelope alive, he blurted out, "She is to me."

At his voice, Penelope ran over and threw her arms around his neck. "Merciful Athena! I thought the beast had come for me."

"In aaaa manner of speaking . . ." Silenus said. "Though I've never *eaten* human flesh. A kiss or two was all I'd hoped for."

Penelope let go of Odysseus and turned to the old satyr. Pulling his head down, she planted a kiss between his little horns.

He let out a contented bleat.

Then Penelope looked over at Odysseus. "Where's Helen? Where's Mentor?"

"They're at the harbor trying to free my old captain and get us a ship."

"Can we get out of here?"

"Easier saaaaid than done," Silenus said. "I've been looking for a waaaay out these past few daaaays. Don't suppose you brought a bit of thread along? So we caaaan see where we've been."

"I could unweave a bit of my dress," Penelope said, holding up the skirt. "It's ugly anyway."

"I'm not sure the Labyrinth will let us go backward," Odysseus said thoughtfully. "But maybe we should be going the other way."

Penelope looked puzzled. "What do you mean?"

"Remember the prophecy," Odysseus said, leaning on the sword. "If we can get the two of you—maiden and horned beast—together in the center of the maze, maybe we'll fulfill the prophecy and get our heart's desire."

"My heart's desire is to get out of here," said Penelope.

"And mine," added Odysseus.

"The center . . ." the satyr said slowly. "Thaaaat maaaay not be so simple."

Before Odysseus could ask what Silenus meant, a horrifying din came echoing through the stone passageways. It was a savage chorus of roars and snarls and hisses, like a pack of hungry beasts.

"What's that?" Odysseus asked.

Penelope shivered. "That's what I thought was the beast until you showed up with Silenus. I've heard that sound three times now."

"It's the real beast," said Silenus. He turned to Odysseus. "Its naaaame is Laaaadon. I've been meaning to tell you aaaabout him."

The awful roars came again.

"You've been *meaning*—"

"Something's coming!" Penelope cried, pointing down the passage, where an enormous shape came slithering out of the gloom.

It was a monstrously huge snake, with a body as thick

as a grown man's waist, so long its tail was still far back in the blackness. Slitted eyes reflected little light, but when it opened its jaws, it exposed a set of long, pointed fangs.

"Take this," Odysseus said, passing the torch to Penelope. "Hold it high so I can see what I'm doing."

He grasped the hilt of the sword with both hands and advanced to meet the serpent. *This is no worse,* he told himself, *than facing a charging boar.* He didn't think about how much larger the snake was than the boar. He didn't think that a light javelin and a heavy sword fit differently in the hand. All he thought about was the danger, and the blood raced wildly in his veins.

The serpent jabbed at him, and Odysseus drew back a step, sword raised. Before the serpent had a chance to try again, Odysseus struck out. Twisting his body around, throwing all of his weight behind the blade as it scythed through the air, he struck downward with the sword, slicing cleanly through muscle and tissue.

Whoosh! he thought. *That was easy!*

The severed head flew into the air like a ball tossed by a child. The body recoiled, whipping back into the dark passage.

Suddenly Odysseus could feel the heat of battle drop away from him, and his knees nearly buckled. He prodded the lifeless head with his sword point. It rolled away, the dead eyes staring at the cave's ceiling.

"That wasn't so bad," he said, pushing the words

out with his last bit of breath. "Like killing any adder. Only . . . larger."

"There's no need to sound disappointed," said Penelope, but her hands were shaking, and the torchlight flickered.

"You don't understaaaand," Silenus said. "Laaaadon's not dead."

Leaning on the sword, Odysseus gave the satyr a quizzical look. "But you just saw me kill him."

Silenus opened his mouth to explain, then gaped in mute horror at something behind Odysseus.

Odysseus whirled around and let out a gasp. There were six more serpents, each as large as the first, hurtling toward them.

Battle fury again surged like a tide through Odysseus' veins. He felt hot and cold and hot. Raising the heavy sword with both hands and screaming, he charged the snaky heads, swinging his sword to keep them at bay.

They rose on their long necks and snapped at him from every direction at once. One of them even curved around behind him and prepared to take a bite out of his neck.

Penelope grabbed the oil lamp from the satyr, lunged forward, doused the snake's head with oil, and set it alight with the torch. The creature let out a screech of pain and pulled sharply away along with its brothers.

"We have to get out of here," Penelope cried, shaking with terror. "We can't fight them all at once."

Odysseus felt the sudden weight of the sword but willed his arms to keep the blade up. "You only mentioned one of these things," he said to Silenus. "Where are all the others coming from?"

"There *is* only one," said the satyr. "Laaaadon—the serpent with aaaa hundred heads. You caaaan chop off as maaaany as you like, but he just grows new ones to replaaaace them."

"You could have mentioned this before," Odysseus said.

"And whaaaat good would thaaaat have done?" asked the satyr. But he was shaking worse than Penelope.

They backed out of the hall, staying clear of the corridors from which the snake heads had come, when a loud snarling hiss to their right caused all of them to turn as one.

Six more snakes were coming toward them.

"Penelope, when I yell 'Now!' we both charge at once."

Penelope gulped and nodded.

"Now!" Odysseus cried. He whipped his sword in a vicious circle, slicing a shower of scales off two of the sinuous necks and cutting a third neck neatly in two. By his side, Penelope jabbed at the other serpent heads with the torch. The five live snakes shrank back from the fire into the shadows, leaving the dead head behind.

"Run!" Odysseus yelled, pointing his sword toward the only corridor that hadn't held snakes.

They spun around and ran down the stone hall, with its bewildering twists and turns. Odysseus led them around a sharp corner, then skidded to a stunned halt.

The way before them was swarming with serpents. Razor-sharp teeth glittered in the torchlight.

One snake lunged forward and ripped the tunic from Odysseus' shoulder. He barely turned away in time.

"The other waaaay!" Silenus screamed, grabbed Penelope by the shoulder, and dragged her with him.

Penelope screamed back as a serpent launched out of a side passage and aimed for her throat. Odysseus knocked Penelope down, and Silenus fell on top of her. Then Odysseus slammed the snake to the floor with the flat of his blade.

"Run! Run!" Odysseus cried.

One by one they leaped over the stunned serpent and ran down the shadow-filled hall. Behind them came the furious hissing of serpents.

"They're everywhere!" Penelope cried. "Everywhere!"

Odysseus knew, with darkening certainty, that she was right.

CHAPTER TWENTY-FOUR

A BATTLE
IN THE DARK

hey raced down the twisting, turning passages. Silenus was in the lead, shouting, "My nose knows."

Odysseus' nose knew nothing. Between the satyr's stink, the musty tang of snake, the damp cave odor, and the nose-drip of fear, he couldn't smell a thing. His arms were both red-hot with pain, his shoulders ached, and terror dogged his heels. Going after Silenus made as much sense as anything.

They ran and ran, panicked, through the zigzagging corridors until they were all out of breath.

Except for their own heaving sobs, an eerie silence filled the Labyrinth.

Odysseus looked back warily. "Have we lost Ladon?"

Silenus didn't answer. His shudder was enough.

Penelope sighed. "Who is this Ladon anyway?"

Taking a deep breath, Silenus said, "From whaaaat the gloating king told me, Laaaadon is one of the maaaany offspring of the giaaaant Typhon and the she-serpent Echidnaaaa."

Now it was Penelope's turn to shudder.

The satyr went on. "Laaaadon terrorized Crete during the early years of Deucalion's reign. There weren't aaaany heroes who could kill him. So they lured him into the Laaaabyrinth."

"And here he's been ever since?" Odysseus had caught his breath. "So why hasn't he starved to death?"

The old satyr straightened. "Oh—he haaaas regular meals. Deucalion sends all Cretan criminaaaals into the Laaaabyrinth."

Odysseus smiled wryly. "No wonder the dungeons are empty and lightly guarded." He glanced at the torch in Penelope's hand. It was flickering now, a sure sign it would soon die.

"Ladon hasn't been giving *you* any trouble," Penelope said. "Both members of the same monster's guild?"

"Oh, he'd eat me soon enough," Silenus admitted. "Snaaaakes love goat meat. But so faaaar I've staaaayed clear of the center of the maaaaaaaaze." His bleating voice let go on the last word.

Penelope sighed. That small bit of breath fluttered the torch. "Too bad. Odysseus' plan to bring us into the center was the only plan we had."

"And it was a good plaaaan, too," said the satyr. "Except for Laaaadon, that is."

"We could sneak past Ladon in the dark, and . . ." Odysseus began.

"His maaaany eyes are shaaaaarp enough to pene- traaaate the gloom of Erebus, the blaaaackest region of the Underworld," Silenus said.

All three were silent, contemplating just how dark such a gloom might be.

"Maaaaybe we should let him eat us aaaand be done with it," Silenus said. Exhausted, he squatted down on the floor.

"Never!" Penelope cried.

"There *must* be a way to kill him," Odysseus added. Though he doubted he'd have the strength to lift the sword one more time, even if they found a way.

"Oh, there is," said Silenus. "But you haaaave to kill his one true head, the one containing his scheming braaaain."

Odysseus leaned over the old satyr and stared at him, eye to eye. "And how do I tell which one is the one true head?"

The satyr's eyes closed. "It's maaaarked, Deucalion saaaaid, with aaaa crimson crest. The others are really just tentacles with eyes aaaand mouths."

"Crimson crest, eh?" Odysseus said, straightening up. "That shouldn't be too hard to find."

"Haaaard enough," muttered Silenus.

"Harder still," Penelope warned, "if the torch goes out."

But having gone through fear and defeat, Odysseus had already come out on the other side. "All we have to do is find the crested head and"—he lifted the sword with a barely concealed grunt—"and I *will* kill him!"

Buoyed by Odysseus' spirit, Penelope lifted the sputtering torch. "You will! You will!" She smiled.

Grateful for her support, Odysseus smiled back and set the sword down carefully.

Silenus got to his feet wearily. "Now Laaaadon's haaaad a taaaaste of your sword, he'll keep his one true head aaaat the center of the maaaaze, well out of your reach."

"The center of the maze!" Odysseus and Penelope said together, and Penelope added, "We're back where we started."

"No, we're not!" Odysseus was suddenly certain. "Do you remember what happened when I cut off that first head?"

Penelope nodded. "The neck disappeared back into the dark."

"Yes!" Odysseus was triumphant. "Just what you'd do if you pricked your finger. Pull the finger away without thinking. Ladon's done the same thing, and *that's* what gives us a chance!"

"I still don't like this idea," Penelope said as they made their way through the dark corridor. The torch was madly flickering.

"We don't have another choice," Odysseus reminded her. "Soon we're going to be completely in the dark. Better to strike when we still have some light on our side."

"We're getting close to the center," said Silenus, touching a finger to his nose. "Laaaadon's bound to attaaaack soon."

"Remember: when he does, you two get away and leave the rest to me."

"I *really* don't like this idea," Penelope said.

Odysseus ignored her complaint. "Lift the torch, Penelope."

She held the torch higher.

They'd come to an intersection of two passages, and Silenus sniffed loudly. Odysseus didn't need any help from the satyr's nose this time. A prickling sensation at the back of his neck had already warned him of the danger.

"He's coming," Odysseus whispered.

"He's here!" Penelope whispered back.

A single serpent body writhed down the corridor to his left. Odysseus turned to face it.

"Here come some more," cried Silenus.

A dozen of Ladon's snake heads, like a great roiling wave, surged toward them.

Odysseus felt the battle fever surge through his body

again and grabbed the torch from Penelope with his left hand. Raising the heavy sword in his right, and heedless of the weight, he rushed toward the snake body.

A hissing head rose to greet him.

With one well-aimed stroke of the sword, he sliced through the snake neck which sent the head twirling through the air. Immediately the bleeding stump whirled back into the shadows.

Odysseus sprinted after it, caught up, and rammed the sword, point down, straight through the scaly hide until it fixed into the thick muscle. Then he wrapped his right arm around the sword hilt.

Now, he thought, *I don't have to raise that awful heavy weight again.* Now, he knew, he just had to hang on.

The snake retreated, carrying Odysseus at dizzying speed along the corridor.

Bang! Into the floor.

Bash! Into the ceiling.

He bounced bruisingly off the walls, his arms and legs scraping over the stones. His arm muscles ached with the effort of keeping his grip on both sword and torch.

At last he was hauled into a huge cavern that could only be the very center of the Labyrinth.

He set down the torch for a moment, and with both hands twisted the sword out of the snake body. It came out more easily than he'd expected, like a knife through meat.

He picked up the torch again. As he did so, he was

immediately aware that everything on his body hurt. He was a single hot point of pain. But he knew he'd have to think about that later.

Now there was only the hero and the snake.

Holding the flickering torch aloft, he looked around. Coiled before him was Ladon's scaly body, as huge as the hull of a ship. Swaying in the air above it was a head twice the size of the others, topped with a bright red crest.

"The one true head," Odysseus whispered.

The narrowed snake eyes glared balefully at Odysseus, and gigantic fangs gleamed like silver swords in the torchlight.

On every side of the body, dozens of elongated necks were thrust down the tunnels. Odysseus was certain they were pursuing Penelope and Silenus, who were weaponless. He hoped the old satyr could keep them clear of the snakes until he finished this task.

If I can finish my task, he thought. Then shook his head. He had to think like a hero. So he forced himself to look up at the head above him and shout, "Come, Ladon, son of Echidna and Typhon, let us see which of us lives and which of us dies!"

Ladon's crested head came straight down toward him, hissing like a waterfall.

Odysseus was so focused on the head before him, he didn't see what was behind. The bloody stump of the neck he'd ridden smacked into his back with the force of a club. The torch fell from his left hand and the heavy sword from his right.

Like a tentacle, the stump wrapped around his waist and hoisted him into the air.

His legs dangled helplessly as the one true head of Ladon drew close. In the last flickerings from the fallen torch, he saw the lipless serpent mouth spread in a cold grin.

He pressed his hands against the coils that were crushing him. He pushed with all his might. But he was a boy—not a man. Even a man could not have resisted those relentless coils.

One by one, the other snakes returned to the center of the maze. They turned their merciless eyes upon him. The crested head was now so close he could feel its cold breath.

Gritting his teeth against the pain, Odysseus clenched empty fists.

If only, he thought, *if only I had a weapon. At least I could die fighting. A hero's death.*

He would never have a song sung about his death. How good it had felt when—in the midst of his grandfather's warriors—he'd told them of his courage in the boar hunt.

"The boar hunt!" he gasped. He *did* have a weapon.

Ladon's jaws were almost over him, the fangs about to bite him in two.

Odysseus reached into the neck of his tunic, pulled out the broken spearhead, yanked it over his neck, and rammed the pointed shard of bronze straight into Ladon's unblinking eye. It pierced the black center, the leather cord dangling.

With a howl of awful pain, Ladon's crested head reared back.

The stump that had held Odysseus loosened with the shock of Ladon's pain, dropping Odysseus. The gold key that had been in his belt clattered to the floor.

He scrambled over to the sword and torch and snatched them both up, surprised that he had the strength to lift either, surprised his legs still worked, surprised that he could breathe again. Then he turned to face the monster.

The cavern was now filled with angry, twisting forms. They swayed and twined around the quivering body, echoing Ladon's pain and rage.

"Come on, you cowardly snake!" Odysseus yelled, forgetting the songs and the stories, forgetting his aches, forgetting how heavy the sword was, remembering only that he'd gotten in a blow. "Fight me now that I'm truly armed. That small point was but a first taste of death. This large point will be your last!"

Goaded by pain, tormented by the boy's arrogance, Ladon's crested head swooped down like a hawk plunging from the sky.

Odysseus braced himself, holding up the sword to meet the attack. And just as the monster's head closed on him, the torch guttered out.

But the momentum had already been set. Ladon's downward motion landed the head onto the upthrust sword. The sword point burst through the soft underside of Ladon's jaw and drove straight through the roof of his mouth.

Odysseus' knees buckled under the impact, and he had to let go of the sword's handle. But the blade was so firmly set now in the monster's head that Ladon's own unstoppable downward movement jammed the hilt onto the stone floor and forced the sharp bronze blade straight into his own brain.

At the moment the brain was pierced, a shriek of agony burst from every one of the monster's multiple heads. His dying cry shook the walls of the Labyrinth and brought dust showering from the ceiling.

One by one the long necks thudded to the floor, and—with a final shudder—Ladon was dead.

CHAPTER TWENTY-FIVE

SECRET OF
THE MAZE

O dysseus crawled out from under the dead serpent and stood up, panting. He could see nothing in the black cavern, but the silence was immense.

Feeling around, he found the crest of the giant head, with the point of the sword like a second crest poking through. But there was no way he could pull it loose. Instead, he felt around till he found the serpent's ruined eye and yanked his broken spearhead free.

Wiping it clean on the hem of his tunic, he put it around his neck again. Then, because his legs were suddenly shaking so hard he was afraid he might fall down, he sat and wept. Out of relief. Out of the lack of fear.

"Odysseus! Odysseus!" It was Penelope's voice.

Suddenly she was there, running toward him, leaping over the dead serpent heads, with Silenus right behind her, carrying the little oil lamp.

She grabbed Odysseus in a fierce hug. "I was so afraid for you."

"Personally," said Silenus, "I waaaas terrified for *us*. We were surrounded by aaaa score of Laaaadon's heads, when they aaaall suddenly let out horrifying screams, aaaand fled."

Odysseus wiped away his tears with the back of his hand, not caring that they'd seen him weep. Then he picked up the gold key that was at his feet and shoved it into his belt. He stood, astonished that his legs could still hold him up. "Now what?" he asked.

"Your plan . . ." Penelope said.

"I hadn't a plan. Beyond killing Ladon."

"Which you did," Penelope said.

"*How* did you do it?" Silenus asked.

So Odysseus told them, quickly, and without embellishments.

They went over to look more closely at the sword embedded in the monster. In the flickering lamplight, the feat seemed even more heroic than it had felt.

Silenus whispered, "We maaaay still need thaaaat sword."

Odysseus agreed, though he doubted he could hold it, even using two hands. He felt that weak.

"Maybe the three of us together . . ." Penelope said.

But it was clear that even three of them could not free the sword from the serpent's head.

However, behind the monster's body, they saw a stone pillar rising up out of the floor. On it were some odd carvings.

"Perhaps that will help," Penelope said. "Perhaps it's the key to our getting out. If it's script, I can read it . . . I hope."

They scrambled over the scaly corpse, but before they reached the pillar, Silenus gasped.

The little oil lamp was finally guttering out, and darkness, like a giant hand, was bent on closing around them.

Silenus cupped his hand around the wick to preserve the last glints of flame for a few seconds more.

"We need something to burn," Penelope cried.

Silenus shrugged. "I have nothing."

An awful thought occurred to Odysseus. Reaching into his tunic, he pulled out the sheets of parchment. They were all that remained of Daedalus' genius, the only chance he'd ever have to build a ship like the master's.

But if we never get out of the maze . . .

He twisted the first piece into a long taper and thrust it into the dying flame.

The flame blossomed between wick and taper, and then the oil lamp died. But the papyrus taper burned clean and quick.

Much too quick.

Odysseus twisted the remaining three pages into tapers, ready for use.

"Let's look at that pillar while we still have light," he said.

They gathered in front of the stone and studied it. It was made up of a series of rounded blocks, each a foot high, and as thick as tree trunks. The carvings reached all the way to the ceiling.

"I can't maaaake anything out of it," said Silenus, his voice a misery.

"*Is* it script?" Odysseus asked. "Can you read it?"

"No," Penelope said, "it's just pictures."

They lit the second taper.

Odysseus walked around the pillar, examining the images, Penelope and the satyr trailing behind him.

At eye level the blocks were carved with pictures of the gods: Ares with a sword, Zeus with a thunderbolt, Apollo with his lyre, Artemis with her bow. Above them were carvings of a ship, a house, a chariot, a vase. Below was a beast half bull, half man.

"The Minotaur," said Penelope, putting her finger on it.

On the same row as the Minotaur were a boar, a fish, and an eagle.

"These must be more than mere decoration," Odysseus said.

"Some kind of story?" Penelope asked.

They lit the third taper.

Taper in hand, Odysseus walked around the pillar again, nervously fingering the key that was stuck in his belt. "We have to think like Daedalus," he said. "We've been in his ship, in his workshop, in his maze. Surely we know how his mind works."

"I don't," the satyr bleated. "But then, aaaall I know of him is this Laaaabyrinth."

Suddenly Odysseus stopped and stared fiercely at the stone pillar. "Take the taper, Penelope. Here—use this last one if needed. I think I understand."

He placed his hands upon the middle set of carvings.

"What are you doing?" Penelope asked.

"It's not a story—it's a key. Artemis, the maiden goddess—"

"And the Minotaur, the horned beast. Of course!" Penelope said.

"I thought I waaaas the beast," Silenus bleated.

They ignored him.

The stones had been set in place for many long years but—as Odysseus had suspected—they were designed to move. He twisted and pushed and, as if grudging any movement, the stone images of the gods began to turn.

Penelope lit the last taper.

"Faaaaster, faaaaster!" Silenus bleated. "The light will go out any moment."

Odysseus was straining with the effort of turning the stone; his hands were rubbed raw. His already aching shoulders protested every turn. But slowly, finally, the figure of the goddess in the stone rested directly over the figure of the Minotaur.

"'When maiden meets the horned beast at the heart of the Labyrinth,'" Odysseus said. "Now let's see about that heart's desire!"

The taper burned out, and darkness held them complete.

Silenus' voice broke the silence. "Nothing's haaaap-pened."

"Wait," Odysseus said.

No sooner had he spoken than a deep rumble filled the dark chamber. There was the sound of huge stones grinding against one another, and a sudden gust of chilly wind blew over them.

"By aaaall the gods, maaaanling, you were right. The Laaaabyrinth is moving."

A whole section of the far wall opened slowly, and light—blessed light—poured in to illuminate a long corridor. Fresh lamps, like the ones in Daedalus' workshop, sprang to life the full length of the hallway.

Then a wall at the end of the corridor opened as well, and beyond it more and more blocks swung open, one after another, as if the blocks were beads on a long string.

Penelope took Odysseus' hand and squeezed. "Shall we follow the master's thread?"

Hand in hand they went down the corridors, with Silenus capering around them. The scent of fresh air drew them faster and faster until they found themselves at last on a grassy hillside far from the city. Above, moon and stars beamed down, as if the gods themselves were smiling.

Odysseus took a deep, cleansing breath. Then he looked back over his shoulder at the gaping tunnel.

"When Daedalus spoke of the heart's desire . . ."

"He meant what every prisoner in the Labyrinth desired," Penelope said.

Silenus understood, too. "The waaay out!" he cried, and his little goat feet beat a happy tattoo into the grass.

For a long while they sat together, luxuriating in the feel of the grass and the smell of the earth and the sound of the wind past their ears.

At last Odysseus stood. Holding his hand up above his eyes, shielding them from moonglow, he looked around. "Over there," he said, pointing.

Penelope and Silenus stood and followed his pointing finger. They saw the silvery sheen of moonlight reflecting on water.

"That must be the harbor," Odysseus said. "If we're lucky, that's where Mentor and Helen and Praxios and Captain Tros will be."

"And if we're not lucky?" Penelope asked.

"Then we're on our own."

"Good luck to you aaaall, then," said Silenus. "I'm off on aaaa different paaaath."

"What's this?" Odysseus said. "Surely you want to get off this island. Come with me to Ithaca. You'll get a hero's welcome there. Wine. Women. Song."

"The only waaaay off this island," said Silenus, shivering violently, "is by sea. I've haaaad enough of thaaaat for one lifetime, thaaaank you. Goats and boats—aaaa terrible mix."

Penelope went over and held the satyr's hand. "But Deucalion will be looking for you."

At her touch, Silenus stopped shivering. "There are plenty of mountains over there," he said, gesturing with his head. "Aaaand mountains mean nymphs. Aaaand wild grapes. Aaaand . . ."

Penelope nodded and once again kissed the old satyr between his horns. "Farewell then, old goat."

Odysseus shook the satyr's hand. "Farewell, indeed."

Silenus turned, stomped his feet, then said over his shoulder, "If you should come aaaacross aaaa jar of wine in your travels, don't forget to toast your old friend, Silenus." With a bound, he was gone.

CHAPTER TWENTY-SIX

THE FINAL CHALLENGE

O dysseus and Penelope found a rough track that led in the direction of the harbor, and followed it down from the hills. It brought them to the outskirts of the city, and they crept through the quiet streets, keeping to the shadows.

Next to the harbor was a large, grotty tavern called the Trident, and inside raucous voices were raised in song.

Crouching low, so as not to be seen through the tavern windows, the two of them passed by. But then a familiar voice called out, "Here's to King Deucalion! And here's to leaving this wretched island on the dawn tide!"

Penelope grabbed Odysseus' hand. "That's—"

"I recognize the voice, too," Odysseus said. "The pirate chief." He peeked over the window ledge.

Inside was the mastifflike chief, and he was surrounded by about twenty of his men. Odysseus saw the three who'd tried to throw him overboard.

Penelope tugged on his tunic, and Odysseus ducked down.

"Who was there?" she asked.

"Your pirates. They're spending their loot unwisely," he said. "Come on."

A little farther on was the quayside, where a dozen ships lay at anchor, illuminated by a sky the color of old pearl.

"Praxios said the slave pens were close by," Odysseus told Penelope quietly.

"There?" she whispered, pointing.

To their left was a brick enclosure locked by a high bronze gate. Dimly visible beyond the bars were a number of sleeping figures.

"But where's Mentor?" Odysseus whispered. "He should have been here long before us."

"And Helen," Penelope added.

As if in answer to their whispered questions, an all-too-familiar voice pierced the air.

"My father and brothers will wage war on this city and burn it to the ground! There are a thousand ships looking for me even now."

Odysseus seized Penelope by the arm, pulling her

behind an empty wagon. Just then Idomeneus appeared around the corner of the slave pen. Behind him were Bosander and four soldiers, herding an increasingly irate Helen, along with Mentor and Praxios.

"Why did you run off?" Idomeneus spun on his heel and addressed Helen. "I've spent all night searching for you."

"I was bored and decided to take a walk," Helen answered snippily. "And what's wrong with that?"

"In the middle of the night?" Bosander said with a growl. "And in bad company?"

"I bumped into them and thought your father had let them go. How was I to know they'd escaped?" Helen continued haughtily, but Odysseus thought he could detect a bit of strain in her voice.

"We told her we'd been pardoned," Mentor put in, but he had no authority in his voice.

He's never been a good liar, Odysseus realized. *Whereas I can tell a tale that everyone believes.*

"Haven't I given you everything you asked for? And kept you safe from the Labyrinth?" Idomeneus was trying to sound masterful, but he kept slipping into unmanly pleading.

"Oh yes, I'm very grateful," Helen said. "And I'm grateful for not being sent to a horrible death like my cousin. If only every Cretan were as considerate!"

She does sarcasm really well, thought Odysseus, suddenly realizing what a good defense it was. Behind her incredible beauty, Helen was not all that sure of herself.

Idomeneus huffed for a moment, then directed his anger at Mentor. "Where's your scheming friend Epicles?"

For a moment Odysseus couldn't remember who Epicles was. Then, biting his lip, he recalled that it was the name he'd chosen for himself.

"Epicles made himself a pair of wings and flew away," Mentor replied stubbornly.

There was a loud *thwacking* sound, and Mentor cried out. Odysseus started to get up, but Penelope pulled him back, silently shaking her head.

Idomeneus' voice, now silky, said, "And what about you, craftsman? We can always put you back in the dungeon. What do you have to say?"

"Being beaten in the dungeon or out, what's the difference?"

Behind the wagon, Odysseus pressed the golden key into Penelope's palm and whispered, "I'm going to create a diversion. While Idomeneus and his soldiers are looking the other way, sneak over to the slave pens and set Tros and his men free."

Before he could leave, Penelope grabbed him by the wrist. "Haven't you taken enough chances?"

"Mentor is my friend. Tros and his men are Ithacans. I can't leave without trying to save them. So just one more chance," he whispered. "If the gods grant it." He grinned at her.

"I was wrong about you," she said softly. "You really *are* a hero."

He looked down and spoke quietly. "I was wrong about you, too." Then he slipped away, ducking through the shadows until he was a good distance from where Penelope was hidden. There he stepped out and walked calmly toward Idomeneus.

"My lord," Bosander said, drawing his prince's attention. "See who comes."

"Ah, Epicles," Idomeneus said, head to one side. "You're wise to give yourself up. It'll go easier on your friends."

"You mistake me, sir," Odysseus said, his hands held out to show he had no sword. "I haven't come to give myself up to you. I've come to challenge you."

Idomeneus raised one elegant eyebrow and moved toward Odysseus. "Challenge? Me?"

"Personal combat, warrior to warrior. If you win, you can do what you want with us. If I win, you let us go free."

"This is ridiculous," said Idomeneus. He glanced at his men. "You've no weapon." He took two more steps in Odysseus' direction.

Odysseus smiled. "Then give me one. Unless you're afraid."

Idomeneus drew his great sword. "This blade belonged to my grandfather, Minos the Great, and has been passed down to me as crown prince of Crete. I won't dishonor it with the blood of a mere boy and a commoner, Epicles of Rhodes."

Odysseus' jaw tightened, and a quick flush of anger lit his cheek. But he calmed himself, remembering that he'd already dispatched a far greater foe. And realizing that he'd probably disgrace himself by dropping another heavy sword.

"I'm no commoner nor am I from Rhodes," Odysseus said. "My name is Odysseus, son of Laertes the Argonaut, prince of Ithaca."

"And a lying rogue to boot," said Idomeneus, which caused his men to laugh aloud.

"Better to be the lying rogue than the fool who believes him," said Odysseus. He grinned impishly.

Idomeneus gritted his teeth. "If you're a prince, then your homeland is going to need a new heir." He took another step forward and raised his sword. Behind him, his men closed the gap at his back.

Odysseus whipped the leather cord from around his neck and held the spear point up. "With this blade, O prince of the Long Island, I slew the many-headed Ladon down in your maze."

Idomeneus laughed. "You do have a certain courage, rogue, though you've said more lies in that sentence than I can count."

"Give me a sword, and I'll show you how much courage I have," Odysseus said.

"Stop it, Odysseus," Helen cried. "He's the greatest warrior in all of Crete."

From the corner of his eye, Odysseus watched the

Cretan guards. Many of them were smiling.

"And how do you know this, Helen?"

She said in loud ringing tones, "He told me so himself!"

Odysseus smiled, too, but didn't relax his guard. "Then let him live up to his boasts." All the while he was thinking, *Hurry, Penelope, please hurry.*

"I don't wish fair Helen to witness your blood on the sand," Idomeneus said. "But you need to pay for your arrogance and lies." He sheathed his sword and un-buckled his sword belt, setting them carefully on the ground. Then he held up his fists.

Odysseus didn't move, waiting to see what would happen next.

"We have a sport here in Crete where we fight with our closed fists alone," Idomeneus said. "Are you up to that, young Ithacan?"

"Do you mean brawling?" Odysseus laughed. He put the spear point on the thong around his neck again. "In Ithaca that's done in the taverns."

"Here we call it boxing," Idomeneus said. "No kick-ing, no wrestling. If you break the rules, you forfeit the fight."

"And if I win, will you set my friends and me free?" Odysseus asked, making fists, though his hands were still raw and painful from the ride on the serpent's back.

"You—win?" Idomeneus laughed, and his men

echoed him. "I'm champion of the Cretan Games," he said, adding casually, "I intend to beat you senseless. As a lesson of course. Merely as a lesson."

Fists raised, Odysseus ran at the Cretan prince and took a swing, but Idomeneus—who was a head taller, though no heavier—stepped easily aside and punched Odysseus hard on the ear.

Knocked off his feet, his right ear ringing, Odysseus took a moment to get his bearings.

The Cretan guards were shouting for their prince, and Mentor and Praxios were yelling for Odysseus. Helen watched through laced fingers, not calling out for either.

If I can keep the fight going long enough, Penelope can free my men. He stood up, shook his head to try and clear it, then closed on Idomeneus again.

This time Idomeneus blocked him with a forearm, and then, as quickly as one of Ladon's heads, a fist thumped Odysseus under the chest and another across the chin.

Odysseus reeled back, throwing his arms up to protect himself. Something salty was dripping into his mouth. He wiped a hand across his lip and he saw blood there.

Keep the fight going, he thought again, then realized that the only way for that to happen was to make Idomeneus come to him.

So he took a few steps back.

Idomeneus followed, as did the half circle of on-lookers.

Then Odysseus took another few steps back. Each step brought the Cretans farther from the slave pens.

"Are you running from me, boy?" asked Idomeneus.

"No more than I ran from the crested head of Ladon," Odysseus said. He saw out of the corner of his eye that Penelope had darted between the shadows of buildings and was heading toward the slave gate. He forced his eyes forward.

Idomeneus took another step, and Odysseus re-treated again.

"It looks like running away to me," the Cretan prince said.

Odysseus had been in his share of scraps over the years, sparring with friends and brawling with enemies his own age. He'd never been beaten. But what Idomeneus had done in those first blows was different than any fighting Odysseus had known. Idomeneus had used his fists like weapons. Odysseus actually admired the man's skill.

But Odysseus knew he didn't need to win the fight. He just needed to hold out long enough for Penelope to free the slaves. Still, he hated being a loser in anything, and he certainly wasn't going to run away.

Entirely sure of himself, Idomeneus was now advancing. Before Odysseus could move back again, he'd taken another couple of punishing blows to the ribs. So he did the only thing he could think of. He wrapped his arms around Idomeneus and held on long enough to recover his breath.

The Cretan finally threw him off and backed away, almost dancing on nimble feet. "Where's your bragging now, Ithacan boy?"

For a moment Odysseus lost his temper and he charged at Idomeneus, who smacked him once again on the jaw.

"Come on, Odysseus," Mentor called out. "You can beat him. Remember the boar?"

All Odysseus remembered was that the boar had slashed him in the thigh. Now his jaw hurt and his ear rang and his ribs were sore, not his thigh. His hands were raw, his arms and shoulders ached. Still, Mentor's cry of encouragement raised his spirits, and Odysseus launched a sudden attack on the Cretan, one blow glancing off Idomeneus' chest, another landing solidly on his chest.

Behind them, Penelope had managed to sneak over to the gate without being seen.

The soldiers called out their own encouragement to their prince.

"He's just a boy!" cried one.

"Finish him," cried another.

"Give him a good one!" cried a third.

Idomeneus, still dancing about like the old satyr on his goat feet, called to Odysseus, "Your strength is failing, boy. But if you surrender now, I'll spare you. You can be my slave, instead of going to your death in the Labyrinth."

Odysseus shook his head twice, then lifted his bruised face to glare at the Cretan.

"What do I care about the maze?" he said. "I told you—I killed the monster. The horned beast and maiden met. I got my heart's desire, which was to get out of the Labyrinth. And as for being a slave—I bow to no man. Not even if you beat me into the ground, Cretan." He spit out a gob of blood.

For a moment, Idomeneus turned away and asked Bosander, "What does he mean about the monster? No mortal can kill Ladon. Isn't that what Father says?"

Bosander shook his head. "He lied before and he's lying now, my prince."

Idomeneus turned back, grinning. "I'm not going to just beat you, boy, I'm going to finish you." He danced over, raised his fist for a massive blow, and brought it down.

But Idomeneus didn't have Odysseus' cunning. At the moment the blow should have landed, Odysseus let his legs buckle as if he'd passed out, and the punch sailed harmlessly over his head.

Then Odysseus stood up quickly, driving his entire body behind his right fist. The fist slammed into Idomeneus' stomach with the power of a battering ram. Every bit of wind was knocked clear of the Cretan's lungs, and before he could recover, Odysseus' other fist crashed into his jaw, sending him flying backward.

Never having been hit solidly before, Idomeneus was overcome with both pain and embarrassment. He lay on the ground, trying to recover both breath and honor.

The soldiers ran to attend their fallen prince as Odysseus slumped to the ground. He was actually in more pain than Idomeneus.

No one noticed that at that very moment Penelope opened the slave pens.

Tros and the Ithacan sailors rushed out of their prison and leaped upon the men who'd enslaved them. Bent over their fallen prince, caught off guard, the Cretans were rapidly overwhelmed by the sheer numbers of former slaves, who stripped them of their weapons.

"Odysseus," Mentor cried, helping his friend up, "you did it!" He handed him Minos' sword, which Odysseus could barely hold up.

Exhausted, one eye closed shut from a blow, Odysseus cried out to Tros and the sailors, "Keep the prince and put the rest of them in the slave pen."

Once the Cretans were locked up, Odysseus went over to the pen and spoke quietly to Bosander. "If you want your prince to live, you'll keep the men quiet."

Bosander's face, with its deep scar over the eye, showed no emotion, but he nodded.

Odysseus returned to his men. "Captain Tros," he said, "time to go home."

"I never thought to see you again, my prince," the old captain said, clasping hands with Odysseus. "I never expected to see Ithaca again, either. But that was better than going back to explain to your father and grandfather about losing you."

Odysseus laughed, then winced. "Laughing hurts. Captain—tell your men that anyone who makes me smile on the way home can learn to swim."

"Do you have a ship then?" asked Tros.

Odysseus nodded. "I have one in mind. But we'd best hurry. I understand the tide turns at sunrise." He pointed to the east, where the dawn's rosy fingers had just reached the shore.

CHAPTER TWENTY-SEVEN

WORTHY FOES

The pirate vessel was as poorly guarded as Odysseus had suspected. The men left onboard were even drunker than the men ashore, and were easily overpowered. Before they knew what was happening, the pirates were heaved over the side of the boat, where they floundered about in the water until finally reaching shore.

Odysseus left Idomeneus on the dock and jumped aboard the ship with the last of his men. As Helen and Penelope settled themselves in the stern, the sailors slid the oars quickly into the water.

Tros saw to the raising of the stone anchor, and the old craftsman Praxios—delighted to be gone from the city—did a little dance on deck.

As the boat began to move away from the dock, the

Ithacans raised a happy cheer. Odysseus looked back and saw that Idomeneus' eyes were fixed on him.

I understand, he thought. Bracing a foot against the stern, with the last ounce of strength he could muster, he flung the silver-studded sword into the air. It landed with a clang at Idomeneus' feet.

The prince picked up the sword and raised it in salute.

"You're a worthy foe, Ithacan prince," he called out. "The best of foes may one day be the best of allies."

Recalling that for all his pride, Idomeneus had behaved with honor toward Helen, Odysseus cried out, "May the gods keep you safe till that time, Cretan prince. Now that your monster is dead, perhaps the Long Island will be a better place for visitors."

"Helen," Idomeneus called, his voice fading in the distance, "I promise I'll see you again, however long it takes."

Odysseus glanced over at the girls. Eyes shut, her head settled on Penelope's shoulder, Helen looked fast asleep. But she was smiling.

The oarsmen rowed well, and soon the boat cleared the harbor rocks and was skimming along.

"Raise the sail!" Tros cried, and when the men had gotten the sail up, it bellied out at once with a strong wind from the south.

"The gods are favoring us at last," the old captain said with gruff satisfaction.

"Those who help themselves, the gods favor," said Odysseus. He started to smile, then raised a hand to his raw face. "Ouch!"

"Best not say that too loudly, lest the gods hear." Penelope was suddenly at his shoulder. She handed him back the golden key. "And let me tend to those wounds. I'm sure the pirates will have a goodly store of medicines."

They searched through the ship's hold and found the fir-wood box that Autolycus had been sending back to Laertes, the one that had kept the boys afloat for so long.

Mentor laughed. "Your father will be pleased to see that!"

Penelope opened the lid, and Mentor let out a low whistle. The box was filled to the brim with gold and jewels.

"This must be the treasure Deucalion paid to buy old Silenus from the raiders," Odysseus said, running his fingers through the loot.

"What does that stinking satyr have to do with anything?" asked Mentor.

"Oh, that's right—you don't know about that," said Odysseus. "Well, better sit down, Mentor, for I've quite a tale to tell you."

"What sort of tale?" Mentor asked suspiciously.

"A true one," Penelope said. "A tale about a monster, a maiden, and a hero."

THE GODDESS SPEAKS

 dysseus woke in the middle of the night, aching all over. But it was not the hard pallet or the pain that had awakened him. It was the light.

Light?

In the middle of the night?

Standing about a foot off the deck in front of him was a tall, beautiful woman in a snow-white robe. The moon shimmered on her helmet, and the point of her spear caught fire from the stars.

"Athena!" he cried. Then he looked around. All his companions were fast asleep.

"They will not wake till I am gone," said the goddess. "I am here for your eyes and ears only, Odysseus."

"I'm listening," he said.

"The gods have tested you, and you have triumphed over all their tricks, as I told them you would."

"The gods?" Odysseus was baffled. "What part did they play in all this?"

"Did you think it mere chance that tossed you into the sea? Mere chance that the mechanical ship rescued you? Mere chance that you escaped from the Labyrinth?"

Odysseus shrugged. "I thought it was ill fortune that dropped me into danger, and my own wits and courage that got me out."

"*I* have been your luck, Odysseus," Athena said. "I sent the dolphins to save you, the warning to flee the workshop. The box, the spearhead, the satyr, the ship, the key—all mine to give."

Odysseus spread his hands apologetically. "I'm sorry if I didn't recognize your handiwork."

"You were not to know," she told him. "You were to find ways to use what you were given. And you proved that the age of heroes is not yet over."

The Age of Heroes. Odysseus grinned broadly. Then, as quickly, he grimaced because grinning hurt, even in a dream.

"And so I can tell you that you will take part in one final great adventure before the Heroic Age draws to a close." The goddess's face was both beautiful and terrible to behold.

Odysseus held his breath, waiting.

"You will sail to a far-off land and fight a long and

dreadful war. Your journey home will be as long and as hard as the war itself."

"You make the adventure sound terrible, Goddess."

Athena smiled. "And who was it who said, 'Any danger averted is an adventure. *If* you live to tell the story.'"

"Will *I* live to tell it?" Odysseus asked, leaning forward eagerly.

"Glory is not won cheaply, Odysseus," she said. "If glory is truly what you seek."

"What else is there?" His face was puzzled.

"A prince can find joy in seeing his people safe and happy, in the love of a good wife, in watching his baby son grow to manhood," the goddess said.

Odysseus shook his head. "Only glory lasts. The bards' songs give us that chance at immortality. Like the gods themselves."

"Think carefully, Odysseus, what you lose by that choice," Athena said. She hefted her spear. "But enough. I know your heart. I know your mind. Enjoy the present. You will have calm seas and favorable winds all the way back to Ithaca. A happy homecoming awaits you."

Odysseus wrinkled his nose at the thought, then drew the golden key from his belt. "And what shall I do with this?"

"Give it to old Praxios," said Athena. "He will need it when he goes searching for his master. Or keep it for yourself. Whichever you do, make certain it is kept away from your grandfather. The gods themselves tremble to think what might happen if a key that opens all locks should fall into his thieving hands." Then she threw back her head and, laughing, disappeared.

Odysseus had never felt so awake in his life. He tapped the golden key against his palm, grinning.

Silenus had been wrong. The gods did have a sense of humor after all.

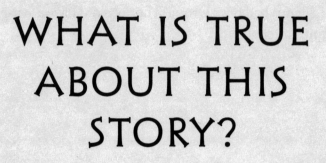

WHAT IS TRUE
ABOUT THIS
STORY?

Did the Heroic Age—the Age of Heroes—really exist?

Yes and no.

No—there was not a time when the gods took part in human battles, nor were there goat-legged men called satyrs or hundred-headed snakes running around the Greek islands. There were no bird-women sirens swimming in the wine-dark sea.

But yes—there was once a rich and powerful civilization in Greece where, though each city was a separate state with its own king, the people were united by a single language. There was also a thriving culture on the island of Crete, and the remains of the great palace at Knossos can still be seen. In that period—we now know from archeological evidence—there was a real Troy and a real Trojan War, though whether it was fought because of the abduction of the beautiful Helen by a Trojan prince is debatable. That great civilization was suddenly destroyed around 1200 B.C.

Five hundred years later, the blind poet Homer created the *Iliad*, a poem about the Trojan War, and the *Odyssey*, about the wanderings of the hero Odysseus. In fact, all that we know about Odysseus can be found in Homer's epic poems and a few Greek folktales. We don't even know whether Odysseus was a real king of Ithaca (or Ithika or Itháki or Ithikai) or just a made-up legendary hero.

All that is related in those sources about Odysseus' boyhood is that he was wounded by a boar on the slopes of Mount Parnassus where he was visiting his grandfather, the cattle thief and robber Autolycus.

But a man—even a legendary hero—must have a childhood and adolescence that foretells his future deeds. In the *Odyssey* and the *Iliad* we learn that Odysseus is a short, burly redhead who is not only a fine fighter but a grand and eloquent speaker. Like all Greek princes, he would have been trained in public speaking, but Odysseus outshines his contemporaries in storytelling. Known as cunning and crafty, he is in fact the cleverest of the Greeks, and not above playing mad when necessary. He is the one who figures out how to sneak out of the Cyclops' cave by clinging to the belly of a sheep. He is the one who teaches his men to stopper their ears so that they might pass by the singing sirens safely. He is the one who invents the wooden horse trick that gets the Greeks (including his ally Idomeneus) inside the impregnable walls of Troy.

Fighter, storyteller, the wily Odysseus wanders ten years around the Mediterranean Sea with his men after the Trojan War as a punishment for offending the sea god, Poseidon. His adventures, as detailed in Homer's epic poem, include gods, monsters, giants, sorceresses, and many a magical happening.

At last Odysseus comes home to his beloved wife, Penelope, and his son, Telemachus, whom he has not seen since the boy was a baby. All those long years her husband has been away, Penelope has kept 108 suitors at bay by her own wits, each night unweaving a piece of cloth she has promised to finish before choosing a new husband. Penelope is aided only by her handmaidens and by her husband's trusted friend Mentor, and her wits are every bit as sharp as Odysseus'.

We have taken the Odysseus of the *Odyssey* and the *Iliad* and projected him backward, using what archeologists have told us about the civilization he would have inhabited if he had been a real man.

Or a young hero.